VICTORIAN MANSION FLOWER SHOP MYSTERIES™

The Lily Vanishes

Elizabeth Penney

Annie's®

AnniesFiction.com

Books in the Victorian Mansion Flower Shop Mysteries series

A Fatal Arrangement
Bloomed to Die
The Mistletoe Murder
My Dearly Depotted
Digging Up Secrets
Planted Evidence
Loot of All Evil
Pine and Punishment
Herbal Malady
Deadhead and Buried
The Lily Vanishes
A Cultivated Crime
Suspicious Plots
Weeds of Doubt
Thorn to Secrecy
A Seedy Development
Woes By Any Other Name
Noel Way Out
Rooted in Malice
Absent Without Leaf
Dormant Lies
Best Laid Plants
Pocket Full of Deadly
To Hive and to Hold

Library of Congress-in-Publication Data
The Lily Vanishes / by Elizabeth Penney
p. cm.
I. Title
2018945965

AnniesFiction.com
(800) 282-6643
Victorian Mansion Flower Shop Mysteries™
Series Creators: Shari Lohner, Janice Tate
Editor: Jane Haertel
Cover Illustrator: Bob Kayganich

10 11 12 13 14 | Printed in South Korea | 9 8 7 6 5 4

1

Fog hung low over the island, drifting through colorful autumn trees like smoke from a nearby campfire. Kaylee Bleu slowed her car to savor the peaceful rural scene. One of the best things about moving to Orcas Island to run her grandmother's flower shop was the commute. No longer did she have to deal with reckless city drivers and congested traffic in downtown Seattle. It was only a couple of miles from cozy Wildflower Cottage, also purchased from her grandmother, to quaint downtown Turtle Cove and The Flower Patch.

This early in the morning most of the downtown businesses weren't open, although customers piled into Death by Chocolate, the bakery owned by her friend Jessica Roberts. Kaylee parked behind the Victorian mansion that housed her own store and got out, holding the door open for her dachshund to leap onto the pavement. "Let's go grab a coffee and say hi to Jessica." She snapped a leash on Bear and slung her tote over her shoulder.

Due to food service regulations, the little dog had to wait outside the coffee shop, tied to a post. Happy to accept the praise of passersby, who adored his cute face and tartan bow tie, he didn't seem to mind.

Jessica greeted Kaylee with a smile. "How are you and Bear today?" She gave the dog a wave through the plate glass window. He wagged his tail, giving her a big doggy grin.

"We're great, thanks," Kaylee said, studying the contents of the bakery case. "I told myself I'd just have coffee but I'm intrigued by those." She pointed to a plate of pretty chocolate confections.

"Those are chocolate swirl meringues." Jessica laughed as

she picked up a sheet of waxed paper. "Very low calorie." She winked.

"I'm sure." Kaylee promised herself she and Bear would take a long walk later.

It wasn't lost on Kaylee that there was an extra bounce in Jessica's step as she filled a to-go cup with coffee and bagged two meringues—one for Kaylee and one for Mary Bishop, Kaylee's part-time employee. Finally she couldn't take it any longer, and she said, "All right, Jess. I know you have something to say. Spill it."

"You caught me. It's huge, Kaylee." Jessica's brown eyes sparkled with glee. "Bernard Martin is filming a movie here on the island. And guess what? I've been hired to cater the set."

"That's great, Jess." Kaylee had heard the name Bernard Martin before. She leafed through her memory banks. "Doesn't he make moody thrillers, like Alfred Hitchcock?" Kaylee remembered visiting her grandmother on wintry Saturday afternoons as a teenager and into her adult years. They'd cuddle up and eat a big bowl of popcorn while they watched one of Martin's movies. The films were spare, elegant, and nail-bitingly suspenseful.

Jessica nodded. "That's right. But this is his first project in years. He more or less retired after his wife died. Now he's back and filming at his compound." She reached out and grabbed Kaylee's arm. "And we're going to be in the credits. You and I."

"We? What are you talking about?" Kaylee regarded her friend with amusement. Never a dull moment with the vibrant, outgoing Jessica around. Maybe she wanted her to help serve cakes at the shoot. That sounded like fun.

The baker leaned across the counter, lowering her voice. "They asked me if there was a local florist who was good. And of course I said yes." She pointed at Kaylee, who gasped. "You and Mary are fantastic. And since the movie is called *Flowers in the Sea*, they need you."

Flowers in the Sea. That was an evocative name. "You're the best, Jess. If they call, I'll definitely do it. It sounds like a wonderful opportunity." She'd never worked on a film set before, and now that it was a possibility, she realized she really wanted to.

The bells on the door jingled and several new customers entered. Kaylee picked up her coffee and bag of pastries. "I'll get out of your way. See you later, Jess."

"Keep me posted," Jessica called. "If Bernard Martin hires you, I want to be the first to know."

Heads swiveled, and Kaylee felt curious eyes on her back as the shop door shut behind her. She stifled a laugh. Thanks to Jessica, rumors of her involvement with the project would be all over the island by the time she finished her coffee.

Juggling her belongings, Bear at her heels, Kaylee unlocked the front door of The Flower Patch. There was still a good hour until the shop officially opened, and Mary had an early morning dentist appointment, so she could sip her coffee and check the inventory in the coolers.

The landline was ringing when she stepped inside, but before Kaylee could get there, voice mail came on. "This is Amy Early, Bernard Martin's assistant. We'd like to talk to you—"

Kaylee lunged for the phone. "Hello? This is Kaylee Bleu. How may I help you?" She ran a hand through her hair, smoothing it in the reflection in the display case as if the woman could see her. Amy began to talk and Kaylee tried to listen and absorb each word. But underneath, excitement swirled in her belly, almost drowning out everything except the basics: She was being offered a huge contract to provide flowers for a real live movie.

"Bernard Martin?" Mary kept a hand on her cheek as she cocked her head in inquiry. Her words sounded somewhat garbled thanks to the numbing agent the dentist had used. "He's back on the island? I never thought I'd hear that."

"Why not?" Kaylee was busy inserting roses into an anniversary arrangement. Next would come baby's breath and greenery.

Mary propped herself on a stool and sipped a cup of lukewarm tea, wincing. "His wife Lily drowned in a pool on their property two or three years ago. She was only twenty-five. He was probably twice her age, but by all accounts he was heartbroken. He left immediately and hasn't been back."

"Until now." Kaylee stripped lower leaves from a branch. "The movie is called *Flowers in the Sea.*" She pointed to a stack of papers on the counter. "Take a gander. Amy e-mailed over the order and a contract."

"Flowers in the Sea?" Behind her designer frames, Mary's blue eyes widened. "But that's the picture he was planning to make with Lily. I understand the script was written for her." She picked up the order and read through it.

"Hmm. I guess he decided to go ahead and make it. Maybe as a tribute to her memory." Kaylee finished the bouquet, set it aside, and started another. "I'm trying to get through these before I leave."

"Leave?"

"It's one of their conditions. They need me to stay on-site quite a lot during initial shooting, to help maintain the flowers or change them if something doesn't look right. I hope that will be okay."

Mary set the papers back on the counter, smiling. "There's no way you can say no to this. It's an incredible opportunity. Besides, it's kind of slow right now, between holidays."

"I should be able to get away if you need me," Kaylee

reassured her. She inhaled, hating to share this next piece of news. She never wanted Mary to feel like she was dumping responsibility for the business on her. "They want me to go out there this afternoon. And get this. They're sending a car for me. Me, Kaylee Bleu, florist."

"And former professor and forensic botanist." Mary reminded her. "That's pretty important stuff right there." Kaylee had worked as a professor of plant taxonomy at the University of Washington, during which time she had also occasionally consulted as a forensic botanist for the Seattle police—work she had unintentionally continued when she'd moved to Turtle Cove.

"I won't need those skills," Kaylee said decisively. "I'm going to a movie shoot, not a crime scene."

A well-kept vintage Lincoln Town Car arrived exactly at three o'clock as promised. "I'll be in touch," Kaylee told Mary, gathering her suitcase, tote bag, and Bear, who had received special permission to join Kaylee.

"Have fun," Mary said. "And promise you'll call me later. I want to hear all about the place. I understand it's incredible."

"I'll do that," Kaylee promised. She tugged on Bear's leash. "Come on, boy. Ready for our adventure?" They exited the shop and walked down the steps to the sidewalk.

A man in a chauffeur's uniform was already holding the back door open. He was short and rather squat, with dark hair and a pitted complexion. He nodded in greeting as Kaylee and Bear approached. "Good afternoon, ma'am," he said in a deep, resonant voice that was so smooth it reminded her of honey. "I'm Mervin Tuttle, your driver. May I take your bag?"

"Thank you. Nice to meet you, Mervin." As Kaylee handed her bag to Mervin to load, she noticed two passengers already inside the car: Jessica and Reese Holt, island handyman and a friend of Kaylee's. Jessica wore a pink cashmere sweater with wool pants while the carpenter had forgone his usual T-shirt and jeans in favor of corduroy pants and a cozy-looking fisherman's knit sweater.

"Reese!" Kaylee exclaimed. "What are you doing here?"

He gave her his heartwarming grin, teeth flashing white against tanned skin. "I've been hired as part of the crew. What a hoot, huh?"

"I'll say." Kaylee slid into the car, enjoying the comfort of the soft leather seat. Bear hopped onto her lap, and Mervin shut the door.

Jessica, sitting on the other side of Reese, leaned forward. "I'm so excited. Mila made me promise to take lots of pictures." Jessica's adult daughter lived off the island.

"And Mary wants me to give her regular updates." Kaylee studied the front of The Flower Patch, admiring the Victorian's gingerbread-adorned charm. A tingle of excitement ran through her body. Oh, how she loved her business and her life here on Orcas Island.

Mervin slid behind the wheel, started the engine, and smoothly merged into traffic. Within a few minutes, they were leaving downtown and heading north.

"Do you know where we're going?" Kaylee asked Reese. They sat shoulder to shoulder, and a whiff of Reese's signature scent—wood dust, cotton, and aftershave—drifted her way. Apparently Bear liked it as much as she did, because he stood up on her lap and nuzzled Reese with his cold nose. "Bear, stop it."

Reese laughed and rubbed the dog's ears. "I don't mind. Bernard's place is south of Deer Harbor."

Orcas Island was roughly shaped like saddlebags, and Kaylee remembered the western side was forked. The western fork was Deer Harbor.

"It's a really cool place," Jessica said. "I checked it out online. It's on its own little island, attached by a causeway." She scrolled through her phone and handed it to Kaylee. "Check this out."

Reese bent his head close to Kaylee's to share the screen, causing Bear to lick his nose.

"Bear!" Kaylee scolded.

"I'll take him." Jessica reached for the dog. "You can't blame him, though." Her eyes were alight with mischief.

Kaylee ignored her friend's remark, but heat burned in her face anyway. Jessica was convinced romance would—and should—blossom between Kaylee and the handyman. Kaylee didn't want to go there right now. She was just happy to have Reese's friendship.

They flipped through the photos, murmuring in amazement at each one. The place was spectacular, a tree-crowned isle with a beach, multiple contemporary buildings, and extensive gardens with charming features. Kaylee noticed they were on a high-end real estate site.

"Is Bernard selling?" Kaylee asked. Realizing that might be an indiscreet question, she glanced at their driver. He didn't seem to be listening and in fact had turned on the radio, which played at a low volume through the front speakers.

"I think at one point he was," Jessica said. "After his wife died. That's an old listing. See where it says 'Not Available' there at the top? I'm glad they left the pictures up, though."

They were well out in the countryside now, and by unspoken assent the trio fell silent, focused on watching the scenery go by. The fog had burned off hours ago, and glimpses of the sound, blue and glittering under the afternoon sun, were visible through the trees. The community of Deer Harbor was charming, with shingled buildings lining the main street. The marina was quite sizable, and even with the chill of early autumn in the air, there were still several boats dotting the water.

Finally they reached the end of the peninsula and, while the road curved up to follow the other shore, the chauffeur turned onto a private road. This led to the causeway Jessica had mentioned. They drove across to an island, where Mervin stopped at a gate. A few taps on the keypad and he was through.

"Fancy," Reese said, his eyebrows wiggling. "A gated estate."

"The price of fame," Jessica said with a casual shrug. "I'm sure Bernard gets lots of unwelcome visitors, including paparazzi."

Kaylee was thrilled at being admitted to the exclusive enclave. She laughed at herself. She was reacting like a starstruck teenager.

The woods soon closed in beside the winding, gravel lane. Within a few minutes, they arrived at what Kaylee recognized as the main house, a sprawling wood-and-glass structure. Mervin pulled around in front of the entrance, although on one side of the circular parking area was a four-car garage. Around the house, sculpted garden areas featured native plants. Right now *Aster subspicatus* were in bloom, shaded by *Cornus nuttallii*, a species of flowering dogwood.

"Here we are," Mervin said, glancing into the rearview mirror. "Welcome to Mukilteo."

"That means 'good camping ground' or 'narrow passage,' depending on who you ask," Kaylee said, recognizing the Native American word and wondering which came first: the estate, or the city on Puget Sound.

"Nice place," Reese said with a low whistle. He eyed the angled structure with its triangular peaks and picture windows. "Post-and-beam construction. Probably all the beams are hand-hewn."

"Hand-pegged too," Mervin said. "Sit tight. I'll let you out."

The driver got out and came around to open the car doors. The trio slid out and waited while he opened the trunk and retrieved Kaylee's bag and two bakery boxes Jessica had brought. Kaylee clipped Bear's leash to his collar and he bounded out, pulling Kaylee behind him.

One of the double front doors opened and a plump woman with a heart-shaped face and close-cropped locks hurried onto the porch. She smoothed a flowing skirt with both hands. "There you are. We're so excited you've agreed to join us."

Despite her warm words, her dark eyes held a touch of sadness, as though some tragedy had touched her deeply. A moment later, she smiled and barreled down the steps, heeled boots clattering. She held out a hand. "I'm Amy Early, Bernard's assistant. And you are?"

"I'm Kaylee Bleu, from The Flower Patch." After shaking Amy's dainty hand, she stepped aside so the others could introduce themselves.

"Let's go in." Amy ushered them up onto the porch. "Bernard is waiting."

"Can't have that," Mervin muttered behind them.

Amy threw him a sharp glance. "Miss Bleu's suitcase is going over to Hideaway." To Kaylee she said, "That's one of the cabins. You'll love it."

"It does sound intriguing," Kaylee said. The idea of staying in her own cabin was appealing too. She liked her privacy.

Amy pointed to a side table. "You can leave those boxes there for now, Mrs. Roberts. Mervin will deliver them to the kitchen."

Mervin, already heading out the front door with the suitcase, gave Amy a salute. "Yes, ma'am."

Bernard's assistant ignored the barb and led the group into a two-story great room with a beamed ceiling, but not before stooping to give Bear a rub on his little brown head. "Your pet is adorable," she said. "I love doxies."

At the far end of the room a gray-haired man of medium height stood in front of a massive fieldstone fireplace, his gaze fixed on a portrait above the mantel. He was dressed in a blue blazer and gray flannel pants, a pair of polished loafers on his feet.

Jessica clutched Kaylee's arm. "That's a painting of his late wife, Lily," she whispered.

As they crossed the polished expanse of floor, Bear trotting along at Kaylee's feet, Kaylee studied the fine painting. A woman with curled blonde hair and pale, delicate features gazed over her shoulder at the viewer. She wore a sea-green gown that faded into a frothy swirl at her feet. *What a beauty.* It was sad that she'd died so tragically.

"Wasn't she lovely?" Bernard said, still staring up at the painting. "We'll try to do you justice, Lily dear. That's the least we can do."

Reese cleared his throat. "Hello, Mr. Martin. I'm Reese Holt. And I'm thrilled to be part of your project."

Bernard gave a start, almost as if coming out of a trance, and turned to face them. "Oh yes. Mr. Holt." A knowing smile played on his thin lips.

What was that smile about? As far as she knew, Reese had never met the producer. Bernard's eyes moved beyond Reese to Kaylee and Jessica. "And who are your lovely companions?"

"They're the florist and baker I found," Amy said, then gave their names and a brief rundown of their qualifications.

"Well done, Amy," Bernard said. He turned to Kaylee and her friends. "Not that I expected anything less. Amy here is a treasure. Welcome aboard, you three. Or should I say four, counting the dog?" He chuckled, then glanced at the gold watch on his wrist. "When are the others arriving?"

"Any minute now," Amy said. "Shall I send Mervin over to

the air strip to collect them?"

"Let's all go," Bernard said. "It will be fun." His eyes lingered on Reese. "A real treat, right, Mr. Holt?"

Reese laughed, but his eyes were uneasy. "If you like airplanes, I suppose." Behind the producer's back, he glanced at Kaylee and Jessica and shrugged. Kaylee couldn't have said what it was, but she had to agree with Reese's unspoken assessment of Bernard. There was something . . . off about him.

Apparently the strip was only a short distance away, located in a field on the estate side of the causeway. Mervin took the car over so he could collect the baggage. Amy rode with him while the rest of them walked, Bernard pointing out features of interest with his gold-tipped cane.

He took them through elaborate flower beds, mostly dormant now, and past a tiled swimming pool filled with blooming *Nymphaea odorata*.

"White water lilies," Jessica whispered. "That is so creepy." She was right. The pool—the one where Lily had drowned?—was now filled with her namesake flower. They were an invasive species, but it was definitely odd that such a thing had been allowed when the rest of the grounds appeared to be fastidiously maintained.

"That greenhouse over there is where we grow rare orchids," Bernard called from his position in the lead. Kaylee and Jessica hurried to catch up. "I'll show you that later, Miss Bleu. We grow some very interesting specimens."

"I'd love to see them," Kaylee said. Her mind began to swirl with ideas. "I'm looking forward to hearing your thoughts on floral design for the film."

"We'll go over that soon. I have preliminary sketches from an artist." He pointed his cane to a path that branched off. "That's the way to the sand beach. Wonderful place. We'll be filming there first."

A jet whined in the clear blue sky, the engine growing louder as it approached. "There they are," Bernard said brightly. He moved marginally faster in the direction of the strip, his cane flashing.

By the time they arrived, the sleek, white aircraft was taxiing along the grass to where Mervin and Amy waited, the trunk of the town car open and ready.

When Kaylee, Bear, and her friends hung back, Bernard gestured them forward. "You must all be part of the welcoming committee. I insist." He waited, hands resting on the cane, while the door opened and the stairs came down.

First to emerge was a striking young woman with strong, well-defined features and short red hair. "That's Tanya Ackerman," Jessica told Kaylee. "She's a really good actress."

"I'm glad you approve," Bernard said, his expression amused.

After Tanya came Randall James, a tall, lean Quinault actor even Kaylee recognized. An older man Bernard called Gordon followed with a thin, tattooed youth lugging camera equipment. Gordon was the director as well as an actor in the production, Kaylee gathered, and the young man, Shane, was the cameraman. They all milled around while the pilot unloaded baggage.

Then a gorgeous, petite young woman dressed in jeans and a halter top appeared at the top of the stairs. Rhinestone-studded sandals sparkled on her feet, matching a headband holding back flowing blonde locks. She stood there grinning.

Reese's mouth dropped open when he saw her.

She came running down the stairs and threw herself into his arms. "Hello, Reese. Surprised to see me?"

2

Who was this lovely young woman, and what was her relationship to Reese? Kaylee didn't care to analyze too closely the feeling that swept over her. *Stop. We're just friends.* Good friends, but still. She had no claim.

Jessica had been chatting with Randall and Tanya, and her glance over at Kaylee and Reese was almost comically alarmed. Kaylee gave her a tiny shrug.

"Kaylee." Reese was talking to her, his arm still around the newcomer. "I want you to meet my cousin Blair. I just learned that she's starring in this movie. Blair, this is Kaylee Bleu. She's the florist for the sets. She runs a flower shop in Turtle Cove called The Flower Patch."

A movie star cousin? Reese was from Los Angeles, so that made sense. "Nice to meet you, Blair." Bear whined at their feet. "This is my dog, Bear."

The actress bent over and patted the dog, cooing. "What a sweetie." Bear's tail all but wagged off.

"I had no idea Blair was going to be here," Reese said with a laugh. He gave her another one-armed squeeze. "I was totally shocked."

"But in a good way, right?" Blair asked, her lower lip thrust out in a pout. "This is a huge break. Bernard has done so much for me." She glanced over her shoulder at the producer, who was busy supervising the loading of the car.

Something in her pose struck Kaylee. *She looks just like Lily.* Finding an actress who resembled the late actress had probably been deliberate, since the film had been written for her. Now

Bernard's remarks to Reese made sense too. He'd known about the surprise.

"I'm sure it is a great opportunity," Reese said. "You'll have to tell me all about it later." Despite his encouraging words, he wore a worried frown while watching Blair sashay over to Bernard.

After kissing his leading lady on the cheek, Bernard waved the cane. "Onward to the beach." Someone groaned, and he said, "Whoever is tired can ride back to the house. But this old man with a cane is going to check the beach. We start shooting tomorrow." After that, everyone except Mervin went along.

The beach was a crescent of beige sand edged by woods and dotted with seabirds. Kaylee spotted tiny western sandpipers, two species of gull, and the common black-and-white pigeon guillemot, which paddled offshore. Bear barked in excitement at seeing the wildlife, and several of the closest gulls took to the skies, sounding the alarm.

Kaylee also noticed a small motorboat trolling the water. Two men were aiming something at the shore—long lenses? *Paparazzi.*

"That didn't take long," Randall grumbled. Standing beside him, Tanya wove her arm through his. Gordon halted on the fringe of the woods. Blair posed coyly, one hand on a hip, pointing a bare toe dangerously close to the cold, frothy water.

Bernard waved his cane. "Take your fill now, because that's all you're going to get," he shouted. The gulls wheeling overhead provided a squawking accompaniment to the producer's outburst.

Even from a distance, they could hear the journalists' laughter. After a few more shots they sped off, raising a wake.

"Blasted reporters." Bernard turned to his cast and crew. "No one is to talk to the press, understand? If this film is going to be a success, we need to control the story." His smile was smug. "They're all salivating for a scoop. We'll make them wait."

Kaylee didn't know much about the entertainment business, but it made sense that the press would be interested in the story. A beautiful actress drowns and her widowed husband decides to produce her final project? Even she could see the appeal.

Gordon, clearly a Californian to the core, shuffled over in sandals with thick leather straps. "Now that I've seen the beach, I was thinking we could set up the cameras near those rocks. Shoot in this direction." He pointed to a cluster of boulders at the end of the curve of sand, then swiveled with his hands in a box shape, as though framing a shot.

Bernard regarded him with narrowed eyes. "All in due time, Gordon. All in due time."

The other man rubbed a hand over his balding head. "Whatever you say," he muttered.

Randall took the older man's arm as he walked by. "Glad you're on board, man."

With a glare, Gordon shook off his arm and didn't reply.

"Burn." Randall waved his hand as if it hurt, making Tanya laugh. He dropped a kiss on the top of her head. *They're a couple,* Kaylee thought. She wondered how serious they were about each other.

As for Gordon, he kept trudging along the sand. Halfway along the beach, he stopped, standing by himself with folded arms. Reese, always the peacemaker, went to join him.

Jessica, standing next to Kaylee, sent her a worried look. Kaylee shared her concern. While not naïve, she had been hoping the assignment would be fun, not rife with interpersonal conflict. *Some customers or jobs are going to be difficult, no matter what.* Her grandmother's words echoed in her head. *So smile and do your best.*

The producer, seemingly oblivious to his director's mood, waved his cane again. "On to the house. After everyone settles in, we'll have a production meeting in the dining room. One hour from now." He began trudging through the sand, the ever-attendant Blair at his side. "Amy, do your magic with food, okay?"

The apparent Jill-of-all-trades watched her boss saunter off with the star, a troubled look creasing her smooth brow. Jessica approached. "Is there anything I can do to help?" She gave Amy a warm smile. "My skills go beyond baked goods. And it just so happens I brought some with me."

"That's right, the bakery boxes." Amy's expression brightened. "I'd be glad to have your help. In addition to helping Bernard, I maintain the gardens and cook all the meals. With the group here, it's going to be a lot of work." She gave a low laugh. "Did you ever end up somewhere in life you weren't planning to go? That'd be me. But I love it here, so I guess it all worked out the way it was supposed to."

Hoping to establish rapport, Kaylee spoke up. "Me too. I used to be on the tenure track at a large university. Now I own a small business on an island."

The rest of the way to the main house, Jessica and Kaylee chatted with Amy about life on the island. Amy didn't talk much about herself, but she displayed the vegetable and herb gardens with pride. "I grow most of the produce we eat," she said, bending to pluck ripe tomatoes from lush green plants. She set them gently in a basket, then reached into her pocket and pulled out a pair of snips. "Cut me a few basil leaves, will you?"

While Jessica cut basil, Kaylee strolled around the herb garden with Bear. Amy had an extensive selection, including climbing purple *Passiflora incarnata*, cheerful yellow *Calendula officinalis*, and pungent *Monarda fistulosa*. The passionflowers, common marigolds, and bee balm, in conjunction with more standard choices, revealed that Amy might be quite sophisticated about herbal medicine.

When Kaylee said as much, Amy said, "I try. I made my own concoction to ease Bernard's arthritis. He says it helps."

Blair popped out from behind a trellis at the edge of the garden, making Bear yip. "Sorry, boy," she said to him. Moving her attention to the assistant, she said, "It's Amy, right? Can you make me a weight-loss formula?" She clasped her hands. "Pretty please." As far as Kaylee could see, Reese's cousin didn't have a spare ounce to lose. *It must be a Hollywood thing.*

"Where'd you come from?" Jessica asked. "You startled us."

The actress waved a hand. "I've been wandering around checking things out. French doors from my room open onto the gardens."

Amy's movements stilled. "Which room is that?"

Blair's smile was catlike. "I think it's called the Sage Suite. And wow, is it nice."

Amy regarded Blair with a tinge of dismay. "That was Lily's room," she said softly.

Clearly Amy had had some affection for Bernard's second wife.

"Hello. Lily is dead." Blair tilted her head, one hand on a hip. "But to answer your question, Bernard put me in there. Any problems with that, talk to him." She swiveled around and stalked off.

With a sigh and a shake of her head, Amy picked another tomato. "I think that's enough."

Kaylee wondered if she was referring to more than the tomatoes.

While Bear watched from a chair across the kitchen, Jessica and Kaylee helped Amy slice rounds of baguette, which were toasted under the broiler, then slathered with goat cheese, tomatoes, and basil to make a delicious bruschetta. A dish of homemade hummus, crisp sliced vegetables, assorted cheeses, gluten-free crackers, and Jessica's decidedly not gluten-free brownie bites made up the rest of the snack spread. They laid everything out on the long table in the great room's dining area. Through tall windows, the water beyond was visible.

"This should hold everyone over until dinner at eight," Amy said. "We're having local salmon with roasted potatoes and fresh mixed greens."

Jessica set a pile of napkins on the table. "That sounds awesome. You really know how to feed people."

"Thank you. I enjoy doing it." Amy smiled, her hands busy with the silverware she was sorting. She glanced at a huge clock on the wall. "It's almost time. Kaylee, would you mind going to fetch Bernard? He has a habit of losing track of time."

"I'll keep an eye on Bear," Jessica said.

Kaylee readily agreed to the errand, happy to have a valid reason to look around the spacious home. According to Amy, Bernard's office was on the lower level, reached by a set of stairs beyond the great room. As she strolled through the house, Kaylee was struck by the elegant simplicity of the construction and decor. Smooth, golden wood was everywhere, accented by cool colors on the walls and in the draperies and rugs. Some people associated beauty with elaborate design. Kaylee knew that often the opposite was true.

Amy had said the office was at the end of the hall. On the way, Kaylee passed several closed doors, and one that was ajar leading to a bathroom. Good to know.

Voices drifted down the corridor from another open door, and instinctively Kaylee's pace slowed. She really didn't want to barge in on a private conversation.

"Don't embarrass me like that again." It sounded like Gordon. Kaylee still squirmed remembering Bernard's blunt dismissal on the beach. "Next time I'll quit."

She halted. *Uh-oh.* She should probably come back later.

Bernard laughed. "You won't quit. Working on a project of

mine is a golden ticket to a career boost and you know that. How many of those have you come across lately?"

Gordon grunted. "Funny that you call it *your* project." His tone was filled with menace. "Be careful, Bernard. Someday you're going to go too far."

3

The office door flew open and the director stalked out, his face thunderous. Kaylee cringed, then managed to pull herself together. She smiled as if she hadn't heard a thing. "Hello, Gordon. I'm here to fetch Bernard—and you—for the production meeting." Surely Amy had meant for her to fetch Bernard and anyone else she happened to encounter.

"Okay." Gordon shouldered past her, and a moment later she heard his steps thumping on the stairs.

Still quivering slightly from the uncomfortable encounter, Kaylee continued on to the end. She rapped on the office door, which still hung open. "Bernard? It's time for the meeting."

"Is that you, Kaylee? Come in."

She pushed the door wider and stood in the doorway. The producer sat behind a massive desk stacked with papers, glasses perched on his nose as he tapped away on a laptop. Built into the slope, this end of the house was far enough above ground to allow a set of sliding doors and full-length windows. Just outside, a small patio sat under spreading trees.

"I'll be right with you," Bernard said. "Catching up on my e-mail." If his disagreement with Gordon bothered him, Kaylee saw no evidence of it. He hit a few last keys with a flourish and shut the laptop, rising to his feet at the same time. Then he fished around on the desk. "I've got something for you."

Kaylee waited patiently as he sifted through folders and stacks of paper, taking the opportunity to peer more closely at the room. Photographs of Bernard with movie stars hung in the wall space between stuffed bookshelves, and on the credenza was a gold-framed portrait of Bernard and Lily. The smiling couple stood near a rose arbor and an unusual modern sculpture. How sad that their marriage had ended in tragedy. Once again, she was struck by the resemblance between Lily and Blair.

Bernard finally found a DVD and held it up. "Aha! Take good care of this. It contains preliminary filming we did years ago on *Flowers in the Sea*." He winked. "Rare footage. Anyway, you'll get an idea of what we want vis-à-vis the flowers."

"Thank you." Kaylee accepted the disc. "This is going to be very helpful."

The producer grabbed a thick book off the desk and tucked it under his arm. "I've got other, newer, better ideas of course," he said, standing back to let her exit first. "As you'll see in the meeting." He didn't use his cane inside, Kaylee noticed. Perhaps he only needed it on the uneven ground out of doors.

Upstairs, they found Tanya and Gordon grazing on the snacks. "Have you seen Randall?" Tanya asked. "I tried his room." She dredged a piece of celery through the hummus.

"Not I," Bernard said. He moved to the chair at the head of the table. "And where's my leading lady?"

The other actress tilted her chin, leveling a glare at Bernard. "Speaking of which, I still don't understand why *she* got the part. I have a lot more credits."

The producer waved that off and picked through the bruschetta on a nearby platter before selecting one apparently to his liking. "Ask Gordon. He's the one who introduced us."

When Tanya whirled on Gordon with such a ferocious glare that Kaylee had to resist the urge to duck. "Really? Is that how it went down?" Her tone dripped malice. "After I—" Noticing Kaylee listening, she clamped her mouth shut.

Gordon tugged at the placket of his polo shirt, his neck reddening. "Well, I, um—" He cleared his throat, then said, "She looks like Lily, that's why. Like the part, I mean."

Tanya folded her arms. "No one can take Lily's place." Her tone was flat. "She was amazing." Her eyes glistened. "And my best friend."

Kaylee darted a glance at Bernard to see how the widower was taking this discussion of his late wife. Busy leafing through the bound book, he didn't seem to hear.

"We all miss her," Gordon said. "But back to the film. Maybe you're not the top-billed star, but your role is great. Meaty, even. I think you might get an Oscar nod out of it."

Tanya's arms loosened and she reached for another piece of celery. "Really? You think so?" She appeared mollified by the mention of a possible Academy Award.

"Absolutely." Gordon nodded like a bobblehead doll in an effort to placate the volatile young woman.

Bernard patted the table. "Why don't you two sit down? If the others don't show up in a few, we'll start without them."

Gordon reached into a bag on the floor and foraged for a notebook and pen. He sat down next to Bernard and scooted his chair in. "I'm ready when you are." He began to turn pages in his leather-bound notebook.

Tanya sat beside him and pulled out her phone. With a flurry of thumbs, she started texting.

Kaylee retrieved her tote from the hallway and sat opposite, which gave her a view of the gardens. She took out a pencil and the notebook she used when talking to clients. She often sketched arrangement ideas on the blank pages. She was hoping to do the same here.

Out in the garden, two figures came into view—Blair and Randall. While she watched, they stopped and exchanged a few words. Then Blair hauled off and slapped Randall hard across the face.

Kaylee gasped. The others glanced at her curiously. She pasted a smile on her face and patted her chest. "Sorry. I choked on a cracker."

"Gotta be careful of those crackers," Gordon mumbled. He bent his head again and continued writing.

She watched Randall put a hand to his cheek. He said something to Blair, and then the duo went in separate directions. *Obviously there's some history there.*

Reese pushed a cart of water, juice, and soft drinks into the room, followed by Jessica and Bear, who ran to join Kaylee. "Where should I park this?"

"How about right here?" Jessica pointed to an out-of-the-way spot. "Can I get you all anything?"

"Is there any coconut water?" Tanya asked, setting her phone on the table.

Jessica searched through the bottles resting in ice. "Yes, ma'am. Amy told me she ordered in a supply of all the crew's favorites."

Gordon tapped his pen on the table. "She's good that way. Very detail-oriented." He slid his eyes to Bernard. "Right, boss?"

Bernard ignored him and popped another bruschetta into his mouth.

Reese pulled back the chair next to Kaylee. "Is this seat taken?"

She smiled up at him, grateful for the air of normality he and Jessica brought with them. "It is now."

Amy, Shane, Mervin, and the stars joined them. First, each person present got a copy of a binder similar to Bernard's. According to Gordon, this was the shooting script, organized according to the filming schedule and locale, not the order in which the scenes would appear in the finished product. Production notes concerning each scene were included.

"All right, everyone," Bernard said. "We're ready to begin. I'll give an overview of the story for those of you who haven't yet read the script." He pushed back his chair and rose, pacing about as he spoke.

"*Flowers in the Sea*. A woman, Blair, married to a much older—and dishonest—man, played by Gordon, regrets her decision and wants to leave him. She has a boyfriend, the foreman of the man's estate, Randall, who is in love with her and wants her to run away with him. Meanwhile the housekeeper, Tanya, who was previously passed over by the husband plots to kill the wife, as does the jealous husband. The boyfriend is killed first. The wife throws herself on the mercy of the groundskeeper, Mervin, who also betrays her and tries to kill her. She must fight for her life—and her sanity."

"It's a thriller," Gordon added. He waved a hand as though conjuring an atmosphere. "Moody, dark, intense."

"It sounds awesome," Jessica said. "I love thrillers."

"Me too," Reese said. "I've seen all your films, Bernard."

Bernard preened. "Give that man a raise."

"In fact," Reese continued. "You're in some of them, Mervin. Am I right?"

Mervin shifted in his chair, obviously uncomfortable in the spotlight. *Odd for an actor.* "Maybe one or two."

Bernard took back the floor by pointing at Jessica. "I want you to design an anniversary cake. Go all out." He demonstrated size with his hands. "Big and elaborate. Lots of frosting and curlicues." He chuckled. "It's going to be destroyed during a fight."

"Between the wife and the husband," Blair added. She grinned, pretending to throw something. "Cake fight." Randall eyed her, his hand going to his slapped cheek, which was still faintly red.

"Bummer," Jessica said. "After all that work." Everyone laughed.

"Sets often get torn down after filming is over, or repurposed," Amy said. "Movies are only an illusion."

"So is most of show biz," Randall said. He picked up his bottle of juice and held it high. "So seize the day, I always say."

"And let someone else pay the piper," Gordon added, lifting his tonic water. "Right, Randall?"

Randall avoided the director's gaze.

What's that about? Kaylee wondered.

After the meeting, Reese accompanied Kaylee and Bear to their cabin, since Jessica was still working in the kitchen. As soon as they were out of earshot of the others, Kaylee said, "Wow. I felt like I was dodging missiles the whole time."

Reese strolled beside her, hands in his pockets. "At least we're not the targets." He grinned. "It's actually kind of amusing. A glimpse into the glamorous world of Hollywood."

"True. And honestly, it's been fun so far." Despite the infighting, the process of taking a story from page to film fascinated Kaylee. Her brain was buzzing with ideas for floral design. She had a copy of the script to read after dinner and, when she was done with that, she would watch the footage Bernard had given her. Her challenge was to use flowers to convey mood and atmosphere appropriate to the film.

They rounded a corner of the path and Hideaway came into view, a wooden cabin nestled under towering firs. Two rockers sat on the front porch, which faced the water, and urns and flower boxes were filled with *Pelargonium hortorum*—bright red geraniums.

Kaylee sucked in a breath. "This is totally charming. I love it." So did Bear, who danced at the end of his leash, eager to explore his new, if temporary, home. She fished in her pocket for the key Amy had given her.

"Here," Reese said. He took the leash, and the pair waited while Kaylee unlocked the door. "This is nice. I'm planning to commute because nothing beats sleeping in my own bed, but

I've been told I can share accommodations above the garage with Shane if need be."

The interior was just as delightful as the exterior, consisting of one big room that featured a stone fireplace and a sleeping loft. In one corner was a kitchenette, and a surprisingly luxurious bathroom was tucked into another, behind a sliding door. The orientation was toward the water, with picture windows providing a vista of late-day sun touching islands in the bay.

Bear, let loose at last, sniffed around the perimeter. As she set her tote on the coffee table, Kaylee noticed her suitcase standing in the middle of the antique rug. She'd unpack later. Right now she was as eager to explore as her dog.

"Look at this." She held the refrigerator open for Reese to see the bottled beverages, cheese, fruit, vegetables, and other types of snack items packed inside. The rustic cupboards held bread, coffee, and canned goods, as well as dishes and cookware. Bernard's hospitality was certainly impressive. Shutting the last cupboard door, Kaylee returned to the fridge and grabbed two bottles of water. "Want to sit on the porch?"

They sat side by side, rocking, watching the sky ease toward night. Bear lay on the porch, his head on his paws, equally content.

"I'm enjoying this," Reese said. "I hardly ever sit down and do nothing."

"Same here," Kaylee said. "Although I love my evenings at home with Bear and a good book."

After rocking a few more minutes, Reese said, "I still can't get over seeing Blair today. Somehow she and the rest of my family kept the whole thing a secret, even when I told them Bernard had hired me. And if you knew my sister, you'd realize how unusual that is."

"It must have been a good surprise," Kaylee said. "I wouldn't mind one involving seeing family unexpectedly." Kaylee's parents lived in Florida, near her brother and his family. Her grandmother, Bea, now lived in Arizona with her twin sister. They were all thousands of miles away.

"It was a nice surprise. She's quite a bit younger so I still remember her being a kid. Now she's all grown up."

"And quite beautiful," Kaylee said. An earlier observation floated into her mind and before she could stop herself, she said, "She's almost a dead ringer for Lily."

"You noticed that too, huh?" Reese leaned his head back against the rocker. "It kind of concerns me, like she's trying to fit into a mold. And she's way too skinny. And sort of edgy."

Kaylee could vouch for the edginess. "Maybe she's hungry. That will do that to people." She decided not to mention the slap in the garden or Blair asking Amy to make a weight-loss drink, as if she weren't slim enough already. "I suppose there's a lot of pressure to be thin."

"I suppose." Reese didn't sound convinced. "Anyway, I'll be keeping an eye on her."

"She's lucky to have you around," Kaylee said. No doubt a young woman navigating the cutthroat world of the entertainment industry needed someone to watch out for her.

"There's something else I learned today," Reese said. Although they were alone, he lowered his voice. "That kid Shane, the camera operator, was gossiping with Mervin." He paused. "Bernard's first wife, before Lily, also died on this property."

"What?" Kaylee rocked forward, startling Bear, who jumped up. "Mary didn't mention that detail to me." She reached down and soothed the dog with a pat. "Sorry, Bear."

"They said it was about ten years ago," Reese said. "Her name was Audrey and she was also an actress. She fell off a cliff while hiking."

"That's awful." Poor Bernard had lost two wives? He had

lived not one, but two real-life tragedies. "Where did it happen?"

"Right here on the property." Leaning forward, he pointed to their left. "Somewhere over there, they said."

"I'm surprised he hasn't sold the place, even if it is fantastic. There must be so many bad memories here." In the direction Reese indicated, Kaylee couldn't see the cliff, but she did notice a glint of glass in the trees, high up. "It looks like there's another building up there."

"There is." Reese reached into his pocket and pulled out a folded paper. "Mervin gave me a map of the property."

He unfolded it and Kaylee scooted the chair closer to peer over his shoulder. The house, airstrip, gardens, and other features were clearly identifiable and labeled. Reese pointed to the square of a building.

"That's the Aerie. Bernard's studio, set on the highest point of land." He ran his finger over the map, landing on Kaylee's cabin. "Here we are. There are a couple more cabins in the woods." He indicated those.

"What's that say?" Kaylee squinted at a spot in the water off the crescent-shaped beach. "'Riptide'?"

"Sure does. It's the way the land is configured. It can be dangerous for swimmers or boats if conditions are right." He laughed. "Or wrong."

The property was full of hazards. Obviously, since two women had died here. "I think I'll avoid swimming and climbing cliffs while I'm here," Kaylee said wryly.

"Good idea." Reese grinned. "Stick to flowers. Those are safe, right?"

Kaylee reflected on all the poisonous plants in the world, some of them quite lovely. Fragrant, even. Kind of like some people who had turned out to be bad news. "You'd be surprised."

Pearly light filled the room and tendrils of fog drifted past the windows. Kaylee, awakened by Bear's insistent nudging, sat up in bed and stared around in confusion. *Where am I?*

Then she remembered. She was staying in Hideaway, a cottage at Mukilteo. The bedside lamp was still burning and the splayed script of *Flowers in the Sea* lay facedown on the cloud-soft, green duvet. She had apparently fallen asleep while reading the script, although what she remembered of it was gripping.

But she'd been exhausted from the day, and stuffed from dinner as well. The meal had been a feast, and thankfully the film crew had put away their sniping for the night. It had actually been fun, listening to war stories about other movie projects. After dinner, Mervin drove Jessica and Reese home while everyone else gathered to watch a selection of clips from Bernard's films.

He was brilliant, no doubt about it. Those who called him a second Hitchcock weren't far off the mark.

Kaylee threw back the covers. "You're right, Bear. Breakfast time." She half-stumbled down the stairs, thankful the loft wasn't accessed by a ladder. She'd have fallen and killed herself for sure.

She filled a bowl with dry food and added a spoonful of wet food, then made coffee while Bear enjoyed his meal.

Two cups of coffee and a shower later, she and Bear were out the door for a morning stroll. The misty air was cool and smelled strongly of salt and evergreens. With the strengthening of the sun, the fog was gradually lifting into the treetops.

Grateful she'd worn a thick fleece, Kaylee moved slowly to soak in the quiet and peacefulness. Strolling under towering Douglas fir trees, it was as if she and Bear were the only ones awake in this seaside paradise.

Then she heard the huffing of someone's breath. Through an opening in the woods, she spotted Tanya, fists pumping as she ran. She had time to notice the woman's strong, muscular arms and legs glistening with sweat, and then she was gone, lost among the trees.

"Impressive, isn't she, Bear?" Kaylee said. They strolled on, taking the path that led toward the beach. Bear loved to run on the sand and chase seagulls.

They passed the lily-covered swimming pool, where Kaylee saw Blair sitting in a tiny summerhouse that resembled a pagoda. She seemed to be meditating and didn't notice them walking by, so Kaylee didn't disturb her reverie.

A short distance later, the path became sandy as they approached the water. The sound of the surf was like music to Kaylee's ears. Bear wasn't the only one who loved the beach.

They stepped between boulders marking the entrance to the beach. Bushes and washed-up driftwood edged the crescent, providing a natural barrier. To one side, about halfway down, Kaylee saw blue cloth flapping in the breeze. Bear barked and pulled sharply on the leash, trying to get to it.

When she got a little closer, she saw it was a man, lying prone on the sand. His blue windbreaker billowed in the breeze, but Kaylee could tell by his utter stillness that he was dead.

4

Kaylee stopped, unable to force her feet to move closer to Gordon. She could tell that it was the director by his balding head and long body. In addition to the windbreaker, he wore khaki shorts and those unique sandals. Grief lanced through Kaylee. *How awful.*

"Hello. What do we have here?" a man's voice said behind Kaylee. She turned to see a stocky young man with straw-like hair and a short beard. He wore a sweatshirt and plaid Bermuda shorts. The camera around his neck told her he must be a reporter.

Great. That's all we need. "I'm not sure," she said. "I just got here." Bear continued to leap and strain at his leash, his barks high-pitched. She tugged at him. "Settle down, Bear."

The young man moved toward the body, taking cautious wide-legged steps across the sand, arms held out at his sides.

"Don't get too close," she warned. "You might destroy evidence."

He glanced back over his shoulder. "You think he was murdered?" He took another step and groaned. "I think you might be right." He reached into his pocket, thick fingers fumbling.

"Don't call 911 yet." Kaylee took out her own phone. Since she was on Bernard's property, he deserved the courtesy of a heads-up about the director's death. She'd stay right here and make sure the reporter didn't take any pictures or mess up the evidence.

"How do you know I was going to call 911?" A mischievous glint came into the reporter's eyes. "Maybe I was going to post on social media that Gordon Hood is dead. That *is* Gordon, right?"

Kaylee waved off his nonsense, quickly punching in Amy's number.

Thankfully she answered right away. "Kaylee? What can I do for you?"

"Amy, I'm so sorry to spring something like this on you first thing in the morning, but . . ." She explained where she was and what had happened. "I wanted Bernard to know first, before I call the police."

Amy didn't respond for a while, and Kaylee sensed she was stunned, which was totally understandable. Kaylee herself was still in shock.

Finally Amy said, "Thanks for letting me know. I'll have Bernard call 911. Hold tight while I go get him. Don't let anyone else near Gordon, okay?" Amy instructed. She made a sound that resembled a choked-off sob.

Kaylee sucked in a breath. *Too late for that.* "Okay." She didn't want to explain over the phone about the intruder. Bernard would have to deal with the reporter, who unfortunately was now a witness. She disconnected. "What's your name?"

He drew himself up proudly. "Jocko McGee, freelance reporter." He lifted his brows, waiting.

"I'm sorry," Kaylee said. "I don't know your work."

His shoulders slumped. "Not many people do. Yet." His fingers fiddled with the camera around his neck as he slid a glance toward Gordon.

"Don't even think about it," Kaylee said. "Bernard Martin is on his way. I'd be thinking instead of a reason why you're trespassing."

Ideas seemed to flicker across his broad face. "I like walking on the beach?"

Kaylee shook her head. "Not going to cut it." She held up a hand. "And you'd better stick around. You're a witness now."

The sound of an engine whining grew closer, and an all-terrain vehicle bumped its way through the gap in the boulders. Mervin was at the controls, with Bernard hanging on behind. They slid to a stop near Kaylee and Jocko.

Bernard slid off, his gaze curious. Then he noticed the camera. "What are you doing here?" Moving with surprising agility, he snatched at Jocko's camera.

The reporter danced away. "Hey, cut it out. There's nothing on here that concerns you."

"That's for me to figure out." Bernard lunged again, without success. "Give me your camera or I'll have you arrested."

Kaylee noticed Mervin was striding across the sand to the stricken director. "Don't touch anything," she called, earning a confused look from him.

"Listen to her," Bernard said. He turned his attention back to Jocko. "I'm serious. The deputies will be here any minute. You're on my property. Without permission."

Jocko shuffled his feet, both hands gripping his precious camera. Then he heaved a great sigh. "All right." He popped open the camera and pulled out a memory card. "You're interfering with freedom of the press, you know."

Bernard's response was a snort. Moving to the water's edge, he threw the chip into the water.

The reporter gave an anguished cry and dug his fingers into his hair. "What'd you do that for?"

"To ensure all your shots are useless." Bernard dusted his hands. "Why else?"

Mervin had joined them again, his skin pale with a sheen of sweat. "How can I help, boss?" His normally mellifluous voice was a croak. "Need me to throw this bum out? We got enough problems right now."

"Nice idea, but the deputies will want to talk to him. Speaking of which, want to go guide them in? They can get closer on the back road." Bernard pointed to another break in the woods further along the crescent.

Mervin hopped on the four-wheeler, made a U-turn in the sand, and sped off. Jocko peered into the surf for his photo card, while Bernard studied the horizon, his gaze somber.

"I'm sorry for your loss," Kaylee said politely. And what a loss it must be for the older man. Gordon was not only Bernard's colleague, he was an essential part of the team on the new project.

Bernard acknowledged her words with a nod, his eyes still fixed on the water. "Gordon was a dear friend. I've known him for many years. He will be missed."

Kaylee unwillingly recalled the argument she'd overheard. At that particular moment, the two men had seemed more like enemies than friends. *Did Bernard kill Gordon?* She'd been so caught up in the shock of finding the director's body, she hadn't had time to speculate about his death.

Bernard was talking again and Kaylee tuned back in to listen. "Poor Amy." He shook his head. "It's never easy to lose an ex under any circumstances."

"Amy and Gordon were a couple?" Kaylee asked. She couldn't imagine a less likely pair, from what she'd seen of them.

"They were married." Bernard waved a hand. "Divorced years ago."

Before Kaylee could ask more questions, she saw a police car bouncing along the trail. It stopped at the edge of the undergrowth, the four-wheeler parking next to it. Two men emerged and she recognized Deputy Nick Durham and Sheriff Eddie Maddox. Some of her tension drained away. They were in good hands now.

Nick spotted her first. "Kaylee Bleu, why do you always beat me to crime scenes?" He strode the rest of the way to her side.

Kaylee cringed, hating how that sounded, though she could

tell he was trying to make her feel better. "I've been wondering that myself."

Bear yipped, recognizing a friend, and Nick crouched down to greet him.

Bernard's brows rose. "What are you talking about, Deputy?"

Durham thrust a hand toward Bernard. "I'm Deputy Nick Durham. And this is Sheriff Eddie Maddox. Miss Bleu here has helped us with a few cases, that's all. She's a forensic botanist."

"Oh I get it. Gallows humor." Bernard shook Nick's hand, then Eddie's. "I'm Bernard Martin. I placed the 911 call." He took a few steps across the sand and pointed. "My director, Gordon Hood, has met with an accident, as you can see."

Nick and the sheriff passed him to reach the body, hunkering down to make an assessment. Nick used his radio to call in reinforcements and forensics, snatches of words drifting toward the small group watching.

Eddie returned first. "We're calling in a full investigative team. At first glance, it appears Mr. Hood died of blunt force trauma, not from an accidental fall. Going by where the wound is and the angle, he was likely sitting on that log when he was struck from behind, but the forensics team will need to confirm."

Kaylee's heart sank. Although she had suspected foul play, hearing the sheriff say it aloud let loose a host of fears. Unless Gordon had been killed randomly, which was extremely unlikely in this remote spot, someone he knew must have done it. Most likely, one of the guests or staff at Mukilteo.

Or a reporter. Maybe one who just happened to reach the scene around the same time I did. Jocko stood at the fringe of the group, shifting from foot to foot, a crease across his young brow.

"Who was first on the site?" Eddie asked, his gaze traveling to each face.

Kaylee raised a hand. "I was walking Bear when we noticed

Gordon lying there. Mr. McGee came along right after. Then I called Bernard's assistant."

"Either of you touch the body?" Eddie barked. "Or trample the scene?"

Kaylee wasn't offended since she realized that he was in full sheriff mode. "No, we didn't. I could tell from here that he was . . . deceased."

"She's telling the truth," Jocko said. "I was walking through the woods when I saw Kaylee out here on the beach. I thought maybe I could talk to her so I came over."

Bernard's eyes narrowed when Jocko admitted prowling around the property, but he held his tongue about that. Instead he said, "Mervin and I left the house right after I called you folks in. When we got here, Kaylee and Jocko were standing in this very spot."

"Are you and Mervin the only two other people on the property?" Eddie asked. At Bernard's headshake, he said, "I'll need all their names, and we'll have to interview everyone today."

The producer groaned. "Really? How long will that take? We were scheduled to begin shooting today. Right here on this beach, as it happens."

Kaylee was disturbed by Bernard's pragmatism. They were going to continue the film shoot even after the director had been killed?

"That's going to have to wait," Eddie said. "This area is a crime scene until we release it. And that means no walkers, no cameras, no nothing."

"Of course, of course." Bernard's lips were a thin line. "I'm sure that sounded heartless, but there's big money wrapped up in this project and—"

"And delays impact the budget." Nick swaggered back to the group. "We get it, Mr. Martin. Or at least I do. I used to live in Los Angeles. Sheriff, can I talk to you?"

Nick and Eddie conferred out of earshot for a minute before they returned. "We're going to move operations to the house once the rest of the team gets here," Eddie said. "But while we wait, Deputy Durham here is going to take statements from Miss Bleu and Mr. McGee. I'll talk to you, Mr. Martin, and Mervin." He pulled out a tablet. "What's your last name, Mervin?"

"Tuttle," was the response.

The sheriff's brows rose. "*The* Mervin Tuttle? Actor in Westerns and action flicks?"

Mervin's pockmarked face reddened. "That's right. I'm retired. Though I do have a part in the new film."

Bernard clapped a heavy hand on Mervin's shoulder. "I only hire the best." His gaze fell on Kaylee. "Like Miss Bleu."

As Kaylee followed Nick to a private spot up the beach, she pondered Bernard's compliment. Had she imagined a warning behind those seemingly innocent words? No matter. She was going to tell the truth even if it resulted in her losing the job. At least she wasn't beholden to the fickle movie industry, like most of the others on the crew. No, plenty of people would need flowers on Orcas long after this movie was finished. Nice, ordinary people.

"So, Kaylee." Nick's eyes were warm with sympathy. "This is one for the books, huh? Take a flower job and the next thing you know, murder."

He really wasn't a bad guy despite his teasing and knee-jerk habit of flirting. Wait until he saw Blair and Tanya. They were both beauties. *And suspects.* She gave a rueful laugh. "It sure is. Where do you want to start?"

His fingers were poised over his tablet. "How about from the beginning?"

Kaylee found herself sharing all she'd experienced and learned since arriving at the property the day before. It felt like it had been a week, with all that had happened. She shared her observations of the various people involved and mentioned the deaths of Lily and Audrey.

Meanwhile, additional law enforcement personnel had arrived. While Giles Akin, the coroner, did a preliminary check of the body, others combed the area for clues.

When she finished, Nick said, "Kaylee, it sounds like you're living in a movie instead of just helping with one. One of those thrillers, maybe."

"Tell me about it." Her earlier cup of coffee was long gone and she was famished. "Do you have any more questions for me? I need a break. And breakfast."

"Yikes, you haven't eaten? Fortunately I think we're done. You can go. You know the drill, though: don't leave Orcas."

"I won't," she assured him.

Kaylee walked Bear through the woods, following a trail that looked like it might avoid the main house and go directly to her cabin. She really didn't want to see anyone at the moment.

After a few minutes, she noticed a flicker of movement through the trees ahead. Someone was headed right for her, on the same trail. For a moment all Kaylee could see was a tall man wearing a blue windbreaker with the hood up and khaki shorts.

The same outfit as Gordon.

5

Kaylee gave a little shriek. Then the figure moved out of the shaft of sun and she recognized Randall.

He grinned, teeth white against his tan. "Sorry. Didn't mean to startle you."

"It's not that," she said. "I thought you were Gordon." His windbreaker had red stitching on the breast, forming the word *Randall's* in sweeping cursive letters.

The actor tilted his head, puzzled. "I don't get it."

Kaylee inhaled deeply. "I'm sorry." She paused. "Gordon is dead. And you're wearing the same—"

"Dead?" Randall's eyes opened so wide the whites showed all around the iris. "What do you mean? Did he have a heart attack?"

"Not exactly," Kaylee said. "He was killed. On the beach. You'd better come with me. The sheriff will want to talk to you. He's talking to everyone," she hastily added.

Randall hesitated. "The sheriff? Wow, this is serious." He flipped back his hood and shook his head to fluff his hair. "I don't know what to do first."

Kaylee began walking again. "There's nothing you *can* do. It's in the sheriff's hands now."

He fell into step beside her and started to ask questions, but she held up a hand.

"I'd rather not get into details," she said. "The sheriff won't like that."

"I get it," he said. He trudged beside her in silence, his chiseled face somber.

Kaylee glanced up at him once in a while. She'd seen him

before in a couple of movies and in guest appearances on television. Since he was Quinault like her, she'd paid extra attention. Now they were alone on a forest path, and she couldn't even enjoy the novelty of their encounter.

He's a suspect too. They all are. That certainly put a damper on her star worship, such as it was.

"This isn't the first time something bad has happened here," he said. "Not to be superstitious or anything, but this is the third death I know of on this property."

"I heard about Lily and Audrey," Kaylee said. "Poor Bernard."

"Yeah, he was pretty beat up over Lily, I can tell you that." Randall picked up his pace a little, as though talking about Lily upset him. "I was here. So were Gordon and Tanya."

Kaylee moved faster to keep up. "Not to sound ghoulish, but what happened? I heard she drowned."

Now that the subject had been broached, his words came out in a torrent. "Lily went swimming every morning in the pool just after dawn. It was her ritual. Poor Tanya found her when she was out for her run. She was devastated. Lily was her best friend."

Kaylee glanced up at the actor. His face was drawn, a hint of moisture in his eyes. "How terrible. For everyone involved." She paused, then asked, "It sounds like Lily was an experienced swimmer. Did they figure out what happened?"

He shook his head. "No. There was an autopsy but they didn't find any physical problems. Just that she did drown. There was water in her lungs."

"It was ruled an accidental death, then?" Kaylee clamped her mouth shut, certain he would think she was interrogating him.

He glanced her way, a curious light in his dark eyes. "You know the lingo. I thought you were a florist."

"I am. But before that I was a university professor and

sometimes consulted as a forensic botanist with the Seattle police."

Kaylee's face heated. While she was proud of her work assisting law enforcement, she didn't like to talk about it. People often got either uneasy or inquisitive.

"Cool. I'll keep you in mind, as a consultant." He studied her, as if assessing her skill. "Production companies often hire people to make sure scripts are accurate."

Not often enough, Kaylee thought, remembering a few mistakes she'd observed. But she didn't say it. "I'd love that, thanks. I was thrilled to get this job."

"I wonder what Bernard will do about the movie now," Randall said, sounding glum. "This project was already put on hold once. Maybe it's cursed."

Kaylee didn't answer. Any announcements about the future of *Flowers in the Sea* needed to come from Bernard.

They reached a fork in the path. "I'm going back to my cabin for a while," Kaylee said. "I'll be up at the house later if anyone is looking for me."

"All right. See you later." Randall turned the other way, striding with purpose.

Kaylee hurried toward her cabin, practically breaking into a run. As it was, Bear had to scurry to keep up with her. The isolated, comfortable space represented sanctuary in her mind. She was thankful to have it, to be able to digest the morning's events in privacy.

While Kaylee was devouring a plate of scrambled eggs and toast, her phone rang. Reese. She immediately felt conflicted. He was one of her best friends, but how much should she say?

But he already knew there was trouble. "Jessica and I were stopped by the deputies just before the causeway," he said. "Are you all right?"

How nice that his first question was about her well-being,

not the murder. "I am, thanks." She swallowed, not wanting to discuss the details. "Did they send you away?"

Reese laughed. "No. Jessica talked her way inside. The big boxes of pastries didn't hurt. We're up at the house now."

"I'll be up after I finish breakfast." Relief loosened tension she didn't even realize she was holding. She wasn't alone here. Reinforcements had arrived.

Up at the house, the guests had assembled in the huge kitchen. It was both an informal wake and a gathering together for comfort. She'd left Bear at the cottage with his toys, dishes of fresh food and water, and a promise to return soon.

Who killed Gordon? Kaylee stood for a minute in the doorway, observing. Tanya, Blair, Randall, and Shane sat at a long oak table drinking coffee in near silence. Amy was at the stove cooking breakfast, her movements jerky and wooden. Jessica and Reese were bustling around, helping.

"Kaylee." Jessica paused and gave Kaylee a one-armed hug, a bundle of silverware in the other hand. "How are you?"

"I'm okay. I'll tell you about it later. What can I do?"

Jessica pointed at the coffee station, which featured a commercial two-pot coffee maker and a gleaming espresso machine. "How about making another pot of coffee?"

"I'll do that." Kaylee detoured to the stove, where Amy tended sizzling bacon. "I'm sorry for your loss, Amy," she said in a low voice.

The other woman regarded her. "Thank you. We divorced eleven years ago, but it still hurts." Only a subtle twitch of her features revealed the depth of her emotion, but it was clear the woman was grieving.

"Of course it does," she said in as kind a voice as she could muster.

As she fit a filter into the holder, she kept an eye on the cook.

Amy's reserve didn't seem healthy, but when Jessica tried to take over, she refused.

"I'd rather do something," Amy said. "I can't just *sit*." Her gaze slid to the group at the table, who seemed quite content doing just that. "Get me some platters, please. This is ready." Jessica found a couple, then followed Amy to the table with plates of the muffins and pastries she'd brought. Kaylee filled a pitcher and poured water into the coffee maker, then watched as hot brew streamed out.

Blair shuddered at the sight of the huge breakfast, although the men dug in. Even Tanya took eggs and one strip of bacon. "I'll just have my green shake, Amy." Blair put a hand to her nearly nonexistent belly.

With a curt nod, Amy went to a cupboard and pulled out a blender. The ever-efficient Jessica began to clean up the cooking area.

Reese frowned at his cousin. "That was kind of rude, don't you think?"

The young actress scowled, folding her arms across her chest. "It's her job."

"And Gordon was her husband," Reese admonished. Kaylee wasn't surprised Reese had picked up that tidbit of information. He was very observant. "Don't make her wait on you hand and foot."

"What's it to you, man?" Randall asked between mouthfuls. He swung his head, shaking his shiny hair into place.

"This is my baby cousin, that's what," Reese said. "And we Holts are raised to be considerate."

Tanya smirked at Blair's discomfort while Shane let out a cackle and turned his attention back to his plate.

Blair continued to pout, refusing to meet Reese's eyes. He moved away and asked Amy what he could do next. A moment later, he was lugging a bag of trash out toward the garage.

Kaylee admired Reese for being genuinely helpful and humble.

The last of the coffee sputtered into the carafe, and Kaylee filled mugs around the table. "I heard you found him," Tanya said under cover of the blender roaring under Amy's watch.

"I did." Something made her add, "Along with Jocko McGee."

Randall reared back, dropping his fork with a clatter. "Jocko? He's bad news." He sent a worried glance at Tanya. "I was hoping he wouldn't follow us here."

"I don't blame you," Tanya said. "He's written some really nasty articles about you." She reached out and patted the actor's arm. "All lies too."

Shane's narrow eyes shone with glee as he dusted his hands. "Case closed. Jocko did it."

"How do we know it wasn't you, Shane?" Blair asked. The malice in her expression told Kaylee she was getting him back for his earlier gibe.

The cameraman's alarm was almost comical. "Not me. I was sleeping in. And where were the rest of you?"

Everyone exchanged looks. Kaylee waited to see if she could tell who was lying. Tanya admitted to her run, but Blair claimed she'd gone for a walk, to get in the mood for her part. She didn't mention being at the pool, Kaylee noticed.

Randall said he was up early reading, then took a stroll. "I ran into Kaylee and she told me what had happened."

The blender finally stopped its grinding, and Amy carried over a tall, frothy glass of something green that reeked of seaweed. Shane held his nose. "Yuck. How can you drink that?"

Kaylee wondered the same thing as she returned the carafe to the heating element. But Blair seemed happy as she sipped the thick liquid.

Bernard entered the kitchen, Mervin behind him. "I'm sure you've all heard the sad news about Gordon. We'll be meeting later to talk about the project, but right now the sheriff wants to interview everyone." Sorrow flitted over his features. Was he remembering the last time an untimely death had occurred here? "I expect full cooperation so we can move on from this tragic event." At Amy's smothered sob, he added, "As best we can, of course."

During the second interview, held in what Bernard called the screening room, Sheriff Maddox sat in. "I know you've gone over all this already, Kaylee," Eddie said. "But it's important to ask questions while memories are fresh." He and Nick sat at a round table near the picture windows. On the wall was the largest big-screen television Kaylee had ever seen outside a movie theater. About twelve recliners were lined up in front of it, making the room resemble a mini theater.

"I understand," Kaylee said. At the moment, she was certain she'd never forget a detail. When she closed her eyes, it was as if the scene on the beach were etched into her brain.

"Was anyone near the victim when you reached the beach?" Eddie asked.

Kaylee shook her head. "No. Gordon was the only person I saw. Jocko came up from somewhere behind me. I have no idea where he was before that." Had he been hiding in the bushes, waiting for someone else to come along, perhaps after he killed Gordon?

She thought about Jocko's camera. "It's really too bad that Bernard threw away the chip card."

"What's that?" Nick asked, his gaze sharpening.

Kaylee played with the cuff of her long-sleeved shirt, realizing she should have mentioned this before. "Bernard made Jocko take it out of the camera. Then he tossed it into the ocean." The words fell into their rapt silence like stones into a pond. To Kaylee, the implications were loud and clear. She'd thought Bernard didn't want photos of the grounds or guests published. But what if the reporter had captured a clue to the murder?

"I'm so sorry," she said. "I should have stopped him from doing that."

"If you could have," Nick said with a shrug.

"In any event, this is exactly the kind of thing we're looking for," Eddie said. "Give us any details you remember, even if they don't seem related to Mr. Hood's death."

The men updated their notes, and then Nick said, "You mentioned that you saw Ms. Holt and Ms. Ackerman on the grounds."

"Yes. Blair was sitting by the pool. The one filled with water lilies. And Tanya was out for a run."

"Coming from which direction?" Eddie asked. He turned a familiar piece of paper to face her. "Show us where both of them were on the map."

Kaylee pointed out the pool and then traced the trail where she'd seen Tanya. It led to the beach, she noticed. *Did Tanya kill Gordon? And did she see me?*

So far Kaylee had felt safe on the property, believing that Gordon's death had nothing to do with her. But if the killer thought she knew something, that put a different spin on the situation.

The two women hadn't been the only people out and about. "I also saw Randall, on my way back to my cabin. That was after I spoke to you, Nick."

The deputy and the sheriff exchanged glances. "Show me," Eddie said, indicating the map.

Kaylee pointed out where they'd met on the path. "This might sound silly, but at first I thought he was Gordon." She laughed nervously. "I couldn't see his face, and they were wearing the same clothes."

"Their windbreakers are similar," Nick said. "Both are labeled *Randall's,* whatever that means."

"Put that on your list to find out," Eddie said. The sheriff slid a plastic evidence bag onto the table. It held a rhinestone headband encrusted with sand. "Have you ever seen this before?"

Kaylee certainly had. "Blair was wearing one just like it when she arrived yesterday."

6

Kaylee stared at the glittering headband in shock. Then common sense kicked in. *Don't jump to conclusions.* Blair hadn't been the only person in the vicinity, and just seconds ago she'd been wondering if Jocko, Tanya, or Randall was guilty. All of them had opportunity, it appeared.

Motive was key, and right now she had no idea why someone had killed Gordon. He seemed to get along with everyone, except Bernard, and the animosity had been from Gordon toward the producer, not the other way around.

"That will be all for now," Eddie said, sliding the evidence bag off the table.

Kaylee was startled out of her thoughts. "I can go?"

"Yes. We're all set for now." Eddie scanned through his notes. "Please send in Jocko. He's next on the list."

As she moved toward the door, Nick called, "Contact us day or night if you remember anything else, okay?" When she turned to face him, his usually lively eyes were somber. "And be careful."

Jocko sat in a chair outside the door, tapping away on his phone. He shifted to hide the screen when he noticed her. "What's up?"

"Your turn. Go ahead." Kaylee began to walk down the hall. Then she halted. "Too bad about your camera card," she said.

The reporter tapped the side of his nose. "One of the first things you learn in news is back up everything."

She wasn't quite sure what he meant, but she was relieved to think that perhaps his photos weren't lost. It was quite possible he'd caught something important, even if he didn't realize it.

Dinner was held around the big table, a buffet on a sideboard offering herbed garlic chicken, roasted vegetables, and salad. The police had left late that afternoon, after the interviews and searching the property. So far, there hadn't been an arrest.

Kaylee sat between Reese and Jessica. "Are you going back tonight?" she asked. She rather hoped they were staying on-site, especially after Gordon's untimely death.

"I was planning to," Reese said. "I have other jobs to take care of." His brow furrowed. "But I can shift things around."

"Me too," Jessica said. "Just say the word."

Kaylee warmed under their concern. "I'll be okay," she assured them despite persistent misgivings. She hated to disrupt their business obligations. "There are good locks on the cabin windows and doors. And I've got Bear." The dog might be small, but he was very protective.

Reese's worried gaze rested on his cousin, who was laughing at something Bernard was saying. "I *will* be staying here later in the week. I want to keep an eye on Blair."

Kaylee hadn't told him about the headband, and holding back the news had been difficult. If it had been her cousin involved, she would want to know. On the other hand, she didn't want to tamper with the investigation for fear of compromising it.

Bernard tapped on his glass. After the table quieted, he said, "I have news. The sheriff has released the beach so we're filming there tomorrow."

After a brief moment of silence, everyone started talking at once. "I will definitely be back as soon as I can," Reese said to Kaylee in an undertone.

"Obviously we're going ahead with the project." Randall's deep voice rang out above the others.

Bernard shrugged. "Might as well, since none of us can leave right now anyway. Make lemonade, as they say. My investors will be happy."

"Does that mean I can't go shopping?" Blair asked. "I need some things."

"Of course not," Bernard said. "They mean we're not to leave Orcas, not this house. Mervin will take you anywhere you want to go."

Blair toyed with her fork, sending a coy look at the chauffeur across from her. "But I don't want to make poor Mervin wait while I try on clothes and poke around shops." She batted her lashes. "That would be so boring, wouldn't it, Mervin?"

Naturally Mervin didn't answer this loaded question. He kept shoveling in food, unlike most everyone else, who only picked.

"You can use Amy's estate car if you want to drive yourself," Bernard said.

Amy didn't appear pleased at this offer, but she didn't object. She got up and went to the buffet table to check the food offerings.

"What's going to happen with the movie, Bernard?" Tanya asked. "Are you directing? And what about the role Gordon was going to play?"

The producer picked up his glass and swirled the liquid. "Yes, I'll take the helm and direct. And I'll act too. I certainly know the script inside and out."

"You aren't bumping me from the love interest role, I hope," Randall said. That got a laugh, easing the tension that had held the room in its grip.

Bernard smiled. "No, I'll be playing the husband."

"As long as what happens on the screen, stays on the screen," Tanya quipped. But she stared pointedly at Blair, a warning in her eyes. Kaylee remembered the scene in the garden between Blair and Randall. Had they once been an item? Was he still trying to get her back, and had his efforts earned him a slap?

Blair tossed her head and laughed, then put her hand on

Bernard's sleeve. "I'm excited to get started. It's an awesome film."

Kaylee was taken aback by the group's eagerness. Did no one mourn poor Gordon? All of these people couldn't be as shallow as they appeared. She hoped. As for her own assignment, she'd better get busy. She hadn't even begun to think about floral design. Murder or not, this was a very important job.

All the same, she definitely would have preferred that there not be a murder.

On the way back to the cabin after dinner, ideas for arrangements began to percolate in Kaylee's mind. In the past, she had found walking very conducive to creative thought, and tonight was no exception. She stopped in the shelter of an enormous fir, absorbing the enchanting atmosphere of a mossy evergreen forest. Somehow she needed to evoke that feeling. Ideas began to filter in. How about tall, curling ferns set off by white, feathery astilbe and bronze calla lilies? She could use real moss as bedding around the plants.

A gentle wind crept through the trees, bringing the scent of salt. Kaylee turned to face the water, enjoying the air on her face. To her left, light filtered through the trees.

What was over there? Kaylee tried to picture the map of the property in her mind, recalling that there were a couple of other cabins close to hers.

Maybe someone was staying in one, although she'd heard the crew talk about accommodations. Blair, Tanya, and Randall were in the house, as were Amy and Bernard. Gordon had been staying there too. As for Mervin, he had a small apartment over the four-car garage, and Shane was staying in the usually vacant studio apartment up there too.

Kaylee moved in the direction of the lights, tempted to investigate. But then a sense of self-preservation overruled the impulse. She'd check it out in daylight hours, when it was safer. And she'd bring her protector, Bear.

Speaking of which, her dog was very happy to see her when she entered the cabin a few minutes later. She'd managed to pop in and out during the day, but he'd been sorely neglected, at least in his eyes. He whined and danced until she picked him up and hugged him.

"Tomorrow you're coming with me," she promised. "But you can't bark while they're filming." She laughed, picturing his little yips in the background of the film. That would get her booted off the set for sure.

Once she had given him the attention he craved—and a treat—she put on the kettle for tea. A soothing herbal concoction was what she needed. In the cupboard were several screw-top jars containing mixtures. *Made by Amy?* She chose the one that promised sleep. She filled a tea ball with leaves and let it bob in a mug of hot water.

Kaylee found the DVD Bernard had given her with the script. She pulled it out of its sleeve and slid it into the slot on the television, one of those all-in-one units. Then she curled up on the couch, Bear snuggled beside her. But before watching the video, she had a call to make.

"News got out that something had happened, but we didn't have any details," Mary said after Kaylee finished telling her everything. "I figured you'd give me an update when you could."

Kaylee smoothed the fringe on a pillow. "I've barely had a moment to myself ever since." Her throat thickened.

Mary made a sympathetic sound. "What an awful thing. Do you think you'll cut the job short and come home?"

Part of Kaylee wanted to do exactly that. But like it or not, she was a witness. And maybe, just maybe, if she stayed on-site, she'd be able to help the sheriff's department. The sooner the case got wrapped up, the better for all concerned.

She set the pillow back against the arm. "Right now I'm staying. If that changes, you'll be the first to know." She took a sip of the tea, which was quite tasty. "So tell me, how are things at the shop?"

Mary gave a full report that put Kaylee's mind at ease and assuaged some of her guilt for abandoning her friend. Kaylee counted herself lucky. There was nothing happening at the shop that the capable woman couldn't handle.

After disconnecting, Kaylee turned on the television and settled in to watch the video. The first shot was a close-up of a white orchid with a bee moving amongst its petals. The film was black and white, an unusual choice but visually stunning. Kaylee could see how it emphasized the sculptural shape of the flower.

She made a note to find out if Bernard was using black and white in this version. It would definitely affect her designs, making shape and structure more important than color.

The video moved on to a clip of Lily lounging beside the Art Deco pool, waited on by a slim and pretty Amy. To Kaylee's surprise, the assistant was a pretty good actress, her face displaying a range of emotions despite the limited role. Randall came into view, passing Amy as she carried an empty tray away. Tanya had Amy's role now. Kaylee wondered what Amy thought of that. Perhaps Bernard had needed to hire someone better known, and after all, Tanya was a rising star.

Lily wore heavy makeup that reminded Kaylee of the 1950s and her hair was styled similar to that of those earlier screen goddesses. Kaylee couldn't tell if that was just a look she liked, or if black-and-white film called for more dramatic makeup.

Gordon, as the husband, interrupted the duo's tryst, and Randall exited. As Lily and Gordon proceeded to argue, Kaylee realized she was watching a rough cut. The camera work was unsteady and erratic, and at one point, swung around and captured a scowling Bernard. He waved the lens away.

Kaylee paused the picture, chilled by the cold anger in Bernard's eyes. This wasn't annoyance at a poor performance or lousy camera work. It was something darker, full of resentment and hate. Who had sparked it?

A realization made shivers run down her spine. *Both of the people on the screen are dead.*

She picked up the remote and clicked off the television. That was enough for tonight. Now she needed to find something light to read, to get her mind off Mukilteo and its tragic cast of characters.

A romance set in Pennsylvania's Amish country fit the bill perfectly. Between the sweet story and Amy's soothing brew, she drifted off with no trouble.

Bear woke her early again, to discover another socked-in morning. After letting him out, Kaylee prepared poached eggs on toast and a pot of coffee. She had slept well, and her creativity had been refreshed, so she made sketches in her notebook as she ate.

A text from Amy told her filming would begin at ten, after most of the fog lifted, which meant she had time to visit the greenhouses and see what was growing there. Anything else she'd have to order from the flower market in Seattle. She went online and browsed the selections.

The tropical exotics were enticing. Depending on the orchids available in the greenhouses, she could supplement them and make compelling displays using some of these. She also loved the market's selection of hydrangeas and dahlias. Both were still in bloom this time of year, so locally sourced.

What should she do for the final scene, when a huge bouquet of flowers was released into the surf? Kaylee scrolled through flower meanings, then came across something so simple it was perfect.

Daisies. They meant purity, innocence, and new beginnings—perfect symbolism for the end of the movie. She pictured hundreds of daisies floating in clear water. What a stunning visual.

Excited now, she made several full-page concept sketches to show Bernard. He was expecting to see them later that day, with the goal of using flower arrangements two days from now. That didn't give her much time to finish the designs, order the flowers, and assemble the arrangements.

After deciding she was satisfied, she closed the notebook and grabbed Bear's leash. Onward to the greenhouses.

Outside the cabin, Kaylee paused, remembering the lights she'd seen the night before. *Should I check it out?* She deliberated so long, Bear tugged at the leash, as if to remind her that he was waiting.

Now was the time to investigate, during daylight hours. "This way," she said, gently leading the dog in the opposite direction from the greenhouses.

She had to hunt for the path, a narrow track that branched off the main loop leading to the house. A narrow depression in the soil was all that marked the way. Thick undergrowth pressed close, which made her think this area wasn't maintained on a regular basis.

Kaylee found a cabin set in a tiny clearing, its peaked roof covered with evergreen needles. Gingerbread trim along the eaves and porch lent a fanciful air, making the building resemble a fairy-tale cottage. But the dirty windows and the dead leaves on the porch were signals that the cabin was abandoned.

"What is this place?" Kaylee asked Bear. His answer was to strain forward, panting, his little legs ready to run and find out.

They covered the rest of the ground quickly. Kaylee halted a few feet away from the building, not wanting to look like she was intruding if someone was inside.

But nothing stirred. The windows remained dark. She noticed a faded sign on the porch beside the front door. *The Lily Pad*, it read in ornate lettering above a cute painting of a frog on a lily pad.

This private retreat must have belonged to the late Lily. Maybe she'd come here to work on parts or just to relax away from the incessant demands of show business.

The fog thickened, wrapping around the cabin like ghostly arms. Kaylee suddenly realized how isolated they were. She tugged on the leash. "Let's go, Bear."

As they moved at a fast clip down the path, she heard a bang. It sounded like a door or window thumping shut. She picked up their pace.

Out on the main path, they slowed, and Kaylee's pulse gradually returned to normal. With a feeling of relieved excitement, she said aloud, "Next stop, the greenhouses." These buildings were near the pool, set in a flat field surrounded by hedges. As she stepped into the enclosure, Kaylee noticed that it was much warmer here, the thick evergreens providing shelter from the sea breezes. But the clearing was large enough that the greenhouses received full sunlight all day.

In the fog, the rows of windows were pearly, faint shadows of green revealing what grew inside. Trimmed grass gave way to gravel, and Kaylee crunched toward the closest one. Anticipation building, she held her breath as she opened the door.

Stepping into a greenhouse was like entering a private garden.

No matter the time of year, it was warm, humid, and full of the scent of growing things.

This building held an explosion of white orchids. She counted at least a dozen varieties, some classic with large beards like *Chondrorhyncha amazonica*, others resembling egret feathers, such as *Dockrillia wassellii inflorescence*. An unusual flower had a fringed lip backed by slender petals. This was *Brassavola David Sander*.

Kaylee wandered slowly through the aisles, Bear at her heels, absorbed by the perfection of the flowers. She paused to admire the delicate *Brassavola nodosa*. Known as the "lady of the night" orchid, the tiny white blooms only released their fragrance in the evening hours. It must be intoxicating when they did.

Movement at the rear of the structure caught her attention. Dressed in yoga pants and a crop top, Tanya was performing a series of exercises, her tan skin damp in the warmth of the building.

"I'm sorry, I didn't mean to intrude," Kaylee said.

Tanya dropped her arms to her side, the intensity of concentration fading from her green eyes. "No problem. I was just about done."

"I don't blame you for spending time in here," Kaylee said. "It's spectacular."

"Lily designed it." Tanya picked up a towel and wiped her face. "She created the collection one species at a time. Having some time to myself in here makes me feel closer to her."

Kaylee studied the closest plants, wanting to ask more but hesitant to probe. "Did she do it for the movie? I saw some orchids in the early test shots Bernard gave me to watch."

Tanya slung the towel around her neck. "Yes and no. The original concept of the film drew heavily on the visual and symbolic aspect of flowers. That was something Bernard has always been interested in, and I think Lily picked up on it." She hunkered down to pat Bear, who licked her hand.

"Who takes care of them now?" Kaylee knew that orchids

weren't necessarily as fussy as people thought, but they did need attention.

The other woman shrugged. "Amy, I guess. She likes gardening, as you can tell." Tanya paused. "But she's no Lily, nor does she try to be. Lily was something special."

Tanya's face was so forlorn that Kaylee had to say something. "You two were close?"

"Best friends, and I'm not just saying that." Tanya's smile was reminiscent. "We met at a cattle-call audition for a television show. Neither of us got the part, but we bonded over the disappointment. Later, when she married Bernard, she made sure I was included in any projects they did."

"That sounds like a real friend." Kaylee had gathered how competitive show business was and how difficult it must be to succeed. Lily hadn't abandoned the other actress when her own star rose. She got the impression that that was a rare occurrence.

"She was." Moisture filled Tanya's eyes, and she blinked rapidly. "That's why I'm going to find out who killed her if it's the last thing I ever do."

7

"You think Lily was murdered?" Kaylee's voice dropped to a whisper. Despite the heat and humidity, a chill ran up her spine. While she'd wondered if the actress's death was suspicious, saying it aloud made it all too real.

For a long moment, the only sound in the enclosure was the dripping of water onto a piece of metal somewhere. Tanya's eyes roved over Kaylee's face, as if deciding whether or not to say more. Then the young woman's expression shut down, and she shouldered past Kaylee. "I have to go."

Kaylee didn't try to stop her. Instead she made another circuit of the enclosure, trying to keep her mind on the orchids. Finally she gave up. Tanya's revelation had effectively broken her train of thought.

After a moment's consideration, she found her cell phone and placed a call. She found a bench against the back wall and sat. Bear slumped to a lying position to wait.

"Good morning, Ms. Bleu. How can I help *you*?"

She groaned. "You're far too chipper for this early in the day, Nick." *And a terrible poet to boot.*

"What can I say?" The squeak of wheels sounded, as if Nick were moving about his office in his rolling chair. "A call from you is as invigorating as a cup of coffee."

Kaylee laughed. Nick's jokes usually cheered her up. "I doubt that." She inhaled. "You told me to call if I had information. I think I might."

"Go ahead." His tone was all business now.

She relayed her conversation with Tanya. "She basically said she's here to try to find Lily's killer. I don't know if the movie gave her an excuse to come back, or if she thought she might as well investigate while she's here."

"And you think her quest might have something to do with Gordon's death."

Kaylee shrugged. "I don't know. Could the two deaths be related? Maybe the answer is in Lily's file."

"Lily's death was ruled an accident." Kaylee heard the sound of papers shuffling. "I happen to have a copy of the case right here."

"That's efficient of you."

"We thought three deaths on the same property warranted another glance through the previous incident," he said, sounding pleased. "Maybe someone missed something the first time. It happens. Or something doesn't become clear until the murderer has struck multiple times and we can pick up a pattern." He hummed under his breath as he flipped pages.

Kaylee stared at the sky through the glass ceiling. She could see patches of blue now, a promise of a sunny day to come.

"Yep, that's what I thought. The autopsy results were consistent with drowning. Water in the lungs, the whole bit. And yes, it was pool water."

"No unexplained bruises or knocks on the head?"

"None. Maybe Tanya is trying to find answers that don't exist. Sometimes an accidental death is just that—an accident."

Kaylee wasn't convinced. After all, Lily had been an expert swimmer. But Nick couldn't just take her word for it. "Thanks, Nick. I'll keep my eyes open and call if I learn anything else. Right now I've got to go watch a movie being filmed."

The rest of the crew had gathered on the beach when Kaylee and Bear arrived. Even Jessica and Reese were already on-site, Jessica in charge of a refreshment table under the trees. Kaylee stopped there first to grab a cup of coffee.

"How are you this morning?" Kaylee asked her friend.

Jessica grinned. "I'm great. This is so exciting. I never thought I'd find myself on a movie set." She nodded her chin to where Shane, Bernard, and Blair were conferring about the first scene. Reese was busy checking the wires running to equipment.

After a few minutes, Bernard declared they were ready to roll. Shane filmed Blair as she wandered along the frothy water's edge, dressed in rolled-up faded jeans and a loose fisherman's knit sweater. Her blonde hair was tossed by the wind in an entirely fetching way.

"How does she do that?" Kaylee whispered. "If it was me out there, I'd look like I was in the middle of a hurricane."

"Same here," Jessica said. She straightened a tray of apple muffins. "Have one of these. They're from a new recipe."

Shane captured Blair walking away, and then took a series of shots of her moving toward him. Next, she sat on a log, pensively gazing out to sea while sifting through sand with one hand. The entire time, Bernard watched a monitor closely, using hand signals to indicate desired changes to angles or distance.

Reese joined Kaylee and Jessica. "This is fascinating, isn't it?" They were standing far enough away, under cover of the surf and wind, to be able to talk without affecting production quality.

"Blair's a natural," Kaylee said. "I'm really impressed by her talent."

"I always knew she was gifted." Reese frowned. "And I can understand the allure of show business. But she's changed. And not in a good way."

In light of the young woman's selfish and often rude behavior, Kaylee had to agree. She gestured for the other two to move closer. "Let's get together later and compare notes." Information related to Gordon's case was still off-limits, especially the headband, but surely they could discuss everything else.

"Sounds good," Jessica said. She picked up a clipboard with the day's schedule. "They're doing a scene in the woods this afternoon but should be done by dinner. How about calling a Petal Pushers meeting tonight?"

Reese didn't usually attend, but this seemed like a good time to make an exception. "That sounds great," Kaylee said.

She pulled out her phone to text Mary, her heart lifting. Things always felt more manageable after consulting the Petal Pushers.

"There you are." Bernard's smile at Kaylee was warm. "I thought we could discuss the floral design over lunch."

Kaylee paused in the act of building a turkey sandwich. Her heart began to thump at the realization that she was about to present her work to be used in a movie. "Sounds good." She glanced around the busy dining room. "Where shall we meet?"

Bernard, who held a plate and a glass, tipped his chin toward the deck. "How about out there?" There was a table with half a dozen chairs and an umbrella sitting near the railing.

"I'll meet you out there." Kaylee finished assembling her sandwich, added chips to her plate, and filled a glass with iced tea. Then she grabbed her tote and made her way outside.

The producer was munching on his sandwich. He wiped his mouth with a napkin and said, "What did you think of this morning's work?"

Kaylee settled at the table. "I thought it was fantastic. Blair has real talent. And I can already tell that this movie is going to have tons of atmosphere."

He crunched on a chip, appearing pleased at her gushing

approval. "I can't deny it. It's a thrill when you take what's up here"—he tapped his head—"and manage to get it on film. The director's vision can be an elusive beast."

Did Gordon share Bernard's vision? The question popped into Kaylee's head, nagging at her. *Knock it off, Kaylee.* Artistic differences seemed like a fairly weak motive for murder. Although when it came to a film, money and reputations were at stake—Kaylee shook her head and forced herself to focus on the purpose of their meeting.

She pushed her sandwich aside, wishing she could eat it since she was starving, and pulled out her notebook. "I've made some concept sketches. If you like them, I'll go ahead and create a list of inventory. I was thinking we'd use the orchids and other plants from the property, then fill in with flowers from the wholesale market. I'll probably go to Seattle and pick them up myself so I can make sure they're in perfect condition." Usually flowers were shipped to her, but she didn't want to risk not getting exactly what they needed.

"That sounds fine." He peered at the first sketch. "Why don't you take me through your ideas?"

Kaylee explained each sketch, trying to convey the look and mood of each arrangement. To her relief, he approved every design. "I'm impressed, Kaylee," he said. "You've taken what we did before to a new level." He ran a hand over the final sketch. "Using daisies for the closing shot is sheer brilliance."

Kaylee's face burned. While she enjoyed receiving praise, she had trouble accepting it sometimes. At the same time, she could see how it might become addictive. Hollywood was a machine fueled by adoration of people and their talents. How far would someone go to stay on top?

One of the sliding doors opened, and Kaylee glanced over to see Mervin emerging from the house. Leaving the door open, he barreled toward their table, hands fisted at his sides. "Boss. The sheriff is here."

Bernard grunted in displeasure. "Again? What does he want?"

Mervin scowled, and Kaylee realized who he resembled—Edward G. Robinson, an old-time actor known for playing gangster roles. "They've got a search warrant for the house and outbuildings. What should I do about it?"

The producer pushed back his chair and stood. "I'm sorry, Kaylee. It looks like our meeting is over." To Mervin he said, "If a judge signed it, we have to let them search. Let's pray they're quick so we can stay on schedule." Leaving his dishes, he moved toward the house with his employee, speaking softly so Kaylee couldn't clearly hear his words. The sliding door slid shut behind them, leaving her alone.

She picked up her neglected sandwich and tried to eat. What were the deputies trying to find? Had they determined what the murder weapon was? She hoped they would figure out who killed Gordon in short order. But if it turned out to be Blair, poor Reese would be devastated.

With a sigh, Kaylee dropped the sandwich on the plate. Lunch was over.

The police operation took hours, so long that filming plans were abandoned for the day. Kaylee witnessed the deputies removing items from the garage before entering the house to search there also. After they checked the kitchen, Kaylee helped Amy and Jessica marinate steak for grilling and making assorted salads. Hopefully the unhappy cast would be able to do the tasty meal justice. One by one they'd circled through the kitchen seeking snacks, lodging complaints with the cooks while doing so. Bernard had put Mervin and Reese to work building sets, with Shane's help.

Bernard, wearing an absurd apron printed with little pigs and an even more ridiculous chef's hat, did the honors at the grill. The evening was warm, the late-day sun touching the deck, so they set the table out there, placing the salads and drinks on a side table.

Tanya joined them last. She plunked a tablet on the table. "Have you seen the news?" At the others' inquiring looks, she said, "We're all over the gossip sites." She used a finger to bring up a story and then showed it around so all could read it.

Deadly Luxury Compound Claims New Victim, the headline screamed. The photograph showed the coroner's wagon driving over the causeway. Another headline read, *Stranger Than Film: Bernard Martin's New Thriller in Real Life.*

With an almost simultaneous movement, all the phones came out of pockets. "What was that site?" Shane asked. Blair and Randall compared notes. Amy and Mervin shared her phone. Bernard continued cutting and eating his steak, seemingly lost in thought.

Jessica, who was sitting between Reese and Kaylee, pulled out her phone too. She made a gesture for them to read along. Most of the articles were brief and stuck to the facts: that there had been a death and the sheriff's department was investigating. But one rag was especially vicious. After starting to read their latest article, Kaylee asked, "Who wrote this?"

Jessica scrolled to the top. It wasn't Jocko, to Kaylee's relief. Sure, he might be a tabloid reporter, but so far he seemed to be keeping a low profile media-wise. Perhaps the sheriff had warned him not to interfere by writing speculative articles like this one.

Blair gave a squeal. "This is horrible, Bernard. How can you be so calm?"

Once again, Kaylee wondered at the self-absorption of these people. They appeared far more concerned about bad publicity than the fact Gordon had been killed.

And that one of them might have done it.

Bernard raised one brow. "Honey, this isn't my first rodeo. I've been around this block before."

She hopped up and down in her seat, unconvinced. "But listen." She read, "'Did renowned director Gordon Hood make the mistake of his life signing on to Bernard Martin's project? That's what some in Hollywood are calling his agreement to work with Martin on *Flowers in the Sea*. Friends say they warned him not to take the job, citing the Machiavellian producer's control-freak habits and failure to give credit where it's due. Now the film's sophomore effort to launch appears doomed by the untimely and suspicious death of Hood, who could have perhaps pulled the fractured pieces of the earlier failure together.'"

Bernard's face had blanched while Blair read, and he held up a hand as though to stop her. But she didn't seem to notice.

"'Now Hollywood is waiting to see if the teetering project can endure this latest blow. Rumor has it Martin himself will take the helm as director. Should be interesting to see if he can succeed without Gordon Hood to lean on.'" She mercifully stopped reading.

"Awesome," Shane muttered, glaring around the table. "Whoever of you killed Gordon really messed things up for the rest of us too." The others flinched at the accusation, glancing at each other with uneasy expressions.

"That's out of line, Shane," Randall said sharply. "There's no proof any of us is guilty."

With a shrug, Shane turned back to his plate of food.

Randall was technically correct. There was no evidence—except for the headband—but the likelihood that a stranger had killed Gordon was extremely low. Perhaps ignoring the ugly truth about Gordon's demise and focusing on the film was a coping mechanism. Otherwise the tension and fear of being trapped here, waiting for answers, would be unbearable.

Bernard cleared his throat. "That article is a load of rubbish. I was already regretting my decision to hire Gordon—"

Someone gasped. *Amy,* Kaylee thought.

"Let me finish," Bernard said with a touch of irritation. "I was going to give the old dog a shot. Anyone remember *King's Kerfuffle*?"

Kaylee quickly looked it up. It was a film directed by Gordon that had bombed spectacularly the previous year. One review team had given it two thumbs down. Others had heaped criticism and abuse on it.

After a few people gave reluctant nods, Bernard said, "Yeah. Enough said. We need to prove these illiterate and ill-informed hacks wrong. I know what I can do. How are you all going to help?"

Blair hopped again, a feverish light shining in her eyes. "I have an idea, darling."

Darling? The endearment had barely registered when Blair began to giggle like a little girl hiding a secret, even going so far as to cover her mouth.

He regarded her with patience. "Do tell. I'm all ears."

"We need to do a press release about the news. You know, *our* news." She wiggled a finger back and forth, indicating herself and the older man. "That will divert the press for sure. The story about Gordon will be yesterday's news."

A wave of shock went around the table as people guessed what she was talking about. Reese swallowed hard, then set his jaw. Tanya glared, while Randall appeared dumbstruck. Amy shook her head, Shane kept eating while darting glances at the action, and Mervin kept his eyes fixed on his boss.

"What's going on, Blair?" Reese said, his voice hoarse. He cleared his throat. "Something positive, I take it?"

His cousin spun in her chair and leaned close to Bernard, her head almost resting on his shoulder. "I'll say. Bernard has asked me to marry him." She bestowed a blinding smile on her audience, happiness sparkling in her eyes. "And I said yes."

8

Randall broke the silence. "Congratulations, man," he said simply. He stood to shake Bernard's hand. "She's a keeper." Others chimed in with their own responses to this less-than-elegant effort.

Kaylee's opinion—even if she had one, since she barely knew these people—wasn't required, so she sat back and watched the interaction. Reese got up and gave Blair a hug, wishing her well. "Wait until the family hears about this," he said with a smile that didn't quite reach his eyes. "You know how excited my mom gets about weddings. And your mother too."

But Blair didn't seem to notice the glares and doubts and half-hearted well wishes. She jumped up from her seat, clapping her hands. "Let's have a toast. Isn't there champagne in the wine cooler?" Then she staggered, putting a hand to her head, and plopped back in her chair. "Ooh. Got a little dizzy there."

Bernard rose to his feet, hovering over her. "Are you all right? Should I call a doctor?"

Blair laughed up at him. "No, silly. I'm fine." She laughed again. "I get light-headed now and then." She tugged on his hand. "Sit."

"She probably doesn't eat enough," Reese whispered to Kaylee.

He was right. From what Kaylee had observed, besides those unappealing green shakes, the actress barely ingested anything. Even at this meal, her plate was full, the food cut up into tiny bites but not eaten.

"I'll go get the champagne," Amy said, pushing back from the table. "You rest a moment, Blair." She walked stiffly across the deck to the sliding door, holding herself in a way Kaylee could only describe as fragile.

"Let's go help her," Jessica whispered. "I think she's upset."

The two of them slipped into the house and through the dining room into the kitchen. The sound of glass breaking came from the kitchen. Kaylee and Jessica glanced at each other and sped up.

In the kitchen, they found Amy staring at a broken drinking glass on the tile floor. She looked up. "I'm so clumsy. I accidentally knocked this off the counter." Tears formed in her eyes and she took a deep breath. "I should clean it up."

Jessica strode over. "I'll get this." She went to the closet and grabbed a broom. Kaylee put her arm around Amy. Tanya barreled in and stood in the middle of the floor with her hands on her hips. "What's up, Amy?" Her eyes narrowed. "Surely this is a happy day for Bernard."

Amy sniffed. "Of course I'm happy for Bernard. And for Blair. It's just . . ."

"Just what?" Kaylee prompted. "You might feel better if you talk about it."

The woman appeared to steel herself. "Gordon and I might have been divorced, but we were still friends. Today would have been our anniversary. And now he's gone."

A wedding announcement on the day of her anniversary? That would upset anyone.

Jessica swept up the rest of the broken glass and deposited the mess into the trash can. "Kaylee, grab some champagne glasses while I wash my hands, will you?"

Kaylee gave Amy a squeeze, then opened the cabinet and began to load crystal onto a tray.

"Thank you," Amy whimpered, using her apron to wipe red, watery eyes. "There should be a couple of bottles of good champagne in the wine cooler. I always keep it stocked."

Arms folded across her chest now, Tanya stared at Amy. "I would have thought you were over him a long time ago. I would have been."

Jessica sucked in a breath. Amy looked stricken and burst into a fresh round of tears.

"Tanya, that was uncalled for. And unkind." Kaylee knew she sounded like someone's mother but she didn't care. How could anyone be so thoughtless?

Tanya just stood there, then said contritely, "Sorry. She's right. That was a terrible thing for me to say. So much is happening around here. I guess my nerves are on edge."

Amy nodded. "I'm going to go lie down. Let Bernard know I'm not feeling well, will you? I'll be all right." She left the kitchen.

Tanya picked up the tray from the counter and carried it out, moving slowly so as not to knock over the fragile glassware. Kaylee and Jessica followed, each holding a bottle of the bubbly beverage.

"That poor woman. I wish we could stay, but I imagine she just needs to cry it out. And we'd better get going," Jessica said to Kaylee. "Otherwise we'll be late for the Petal Pushers meeting."

"Okay," Kaylee said. She'd been looking forward to seeing Mary and DeeDee, who also belonged to the club, all day. She needed the breath of fresh air their friendship provided.

"I think I'll spend the night at home," she told Jessica, feeling relief at escaping the island even briefly while a killer was on the loose. "Tomorrow I'll bring my own car back here." She'd be doing a lot of back and forth once shooting was fully underway. The flower arrangements would need to be either created or freshened daily.

After the toast, during which Reese abstained from drinking the champagne, they drove out of the compound in his truck.

Kaylee and Bear were in the front seat at Jessica's insistence, while she sat in the smaller back seat.

They rode in silence for a few minutes, each lost in their thoughts. Kaylee watched the moon rise over the ocean, a pale disk in a field of indigo.

"I still can't believe it," Reese said. He drove in his usual alert-yet-relaxed fashion, an elbow on the window ledge, his eyes fixed on the road ahead. "I knew he was some kind of mentor, but wow. Marry the guy? He's three times her age."

"To be fair, he is charming, handsome, and highly accomplished," Kaylee said. "That can be attractive to a young woman." Especially one seeking a solid footing in a very unstable industry like show business.

"It seems like a mutually beneficial situation to me," Jessica said from the back. "He's got the experience and connections, and she's got the talent. They could be the next Hollywood power couple." She thought for a minute. "But I can't think of a cute blended name for them."

"I'm glad of that," Reese said, rolling his eyes. "I hate those corny couple names."

In response, Jessica threw out a few ridiculous options—including "Blernard" and "Bernair"—which made them laugh.

When they pulled into the parking lot at the Old Cape Lighthouse, Mary and DeeDee's cars were already there. "Sure it's okay if I crash the meeting?" Reese asked. "I don't want to intrude."

"No, please join us," Kaylee said. "I have a feeling we're going to be spending most of our time talking about the film project."

They entered the former living quarters at the lighthouse, the usual meeting place, and found not only an array of refreshments, but a pile of thick manila folders on the table.

After greetings and hugs were exchanged, Kaylee asked,

"What's in those folders?"

DeeDee grinned. "I took the time to make dossiers on each of the people involved with your movie." She picked up the top one, marked *Bernard*, and handed it to Kaylee. "I thought these might help with the case." She passed out the rest to the others, who took seats around the table.

Kaylee opened the folder, which contained a series of colorful articles from tabloid newspapers and gossip magazines. "I guess the sheriff's department has its methods and we Petal Pushers have ours."

"Don't knock it," Mary said, tapping her finger on a file. "There's usually a nugget of truth in these articles even if they are sensationalized."

"I picked the most reputable publications," DeeDee said. "No alien abductions or ghost stories."

Jessica, who was a fan of conspiracy theories, snapped her fingers. "Too bad. I love those." She had the folders on Tanya and Blair, both relative newcomers to show business. DeeDee assigned Gordon and Amy to Mary, Reese had the one on Mervin, and DeeDee took Randall.

"What I thought we'd do is go through and pull out any articles that seem to relate to the case now," DeeDee said. "I printed everything I could find, including bios and filmographies. But those are good background."

"I suggest we look for information about Lily's and Audrey's deaths too," Kaylee suggested. "Tanya told me she's trying to find Lily's killer." At the gasps from everyone, she realized she hadn't even mentioned the greenhouse conversation to Reese and Jessica.

"You've been holding out on us, lady," Jessica scolded. "Any other tidbits we should know about?"

The headband flashed into Kaylee's mind, but she refrained

once again from mentioning it. "I'm sorry. I meant to tell you but it was so hectic today."

"Yeah, what with a search warrant being executed and my cousin getting engaged." Reese's tone was dry.

"Blair's engaged? To whom?" Mary asked.

Reese made a helpless gesture, obviously not wanting to discuss it, so Kaylee filled them in. "Don't say a word to anyone. I think they're planning a big media announcement tomorrow."

DeeDee made a zipping motion across her mouth. "No one will hear it from me. But wow, is it ever hard sitting on something like that."

"Try," Kaylee urged. "Anyway, how about we give a little update before we read so everyone is on the same page?"

The trio filled Mary and DeeDee in on everything that had happened at Mukilteo over the past few days. "I can't help but feel that the solution to Gordon's murder is in the past, in the relationships among that group," Kaylee concluded.

"And I can't help but *know* that Blair is in over her head," Reese added. "She's like a minnow swimming with the sharks."

Mary studied Reese, sympathy etched on her features. "She's lucky to have such a protective older cousin."

He scoffed. "Big help I've been. A man was killed right under everyone's nose. And now she's engaged to a man who's outlived two wives."

"And not only that, his former wives both died at a young age." DeeDee's voice was somber. "We've got to get to the bottom of this, for Blair's sake."

On that grim note, everyone began to leaf through their folders, searching for clues and information to shed light on the players. DeeDee suggested that they each take notes and then share with the group after going through the files.

An hour later, Jessica put down her pen. "I'm done."

They all agreed. "Who should go first?" Mary asked.

"How about Kaylee?" DeeDee suggested. "Since she was assigned the big kahuna."

"He certainly seems to be the linchpin bringing everyone together," Kaylee said. She glanced through her notes. "All right. Bernard Martin has made over thirty films and has received two Academy Awards. His most famous film starred his first wife, Audrey." She held up Exhibit A, a picture of Audrey and Bernard at their wedding, with much younger and trimmer Amy and Gordon as attendants. Audrey was a petite blonde, like Lily and Blair. Kaylee named a few of her movies.

"I've seen all of those," Mary said. "She was very gifted."

Kaylee went on. "There were rumors of trouble in paradise, though." She showed them articles claiming Bernard and Audrey experienced very volatile incidents during their marriage. "According to this story, Audrey was seeking a divorce."

"Right around the time she fell off that cliff," Mary guessed.

"That happened soon after the divorce rumors were printed," Kaylee confirmed. "Bernard's career faltered for a while after Audrey died. Then he started working with Lily, who was an unknown. *Tiny Boxes*, a film starring her, was a surprise box-office smash and a festival award winner. Then two years ago, she drowned. Again, after rumors of divorce. Now they call him the 'Black Widower.'"

Reese scrubbed his face with both hands and groaned. "I've got to get Blair out of there. There's a pattern." He ticked off points on his fingers. "Unknown but talented beauty. Rising stardom with Bernard's help. Disillusionment for whatever reason. And then they—you know."

He didn't need to finish the statement. Kaylee had come to the same conclusion, that there were uncanny—and dangerous—similarities between the women's careers and relationships with

Bernard. But she wasn't quite ready to make the leap between Bernard and Gordon's death. "Maybe by figuring out who killed Gordon, we'll shed some light on the other deaths," she said. "Who's next?"

Mary raised her hand. "I've got Gordon, so I'll go ahead." She glanced over her notes. "The first thing is, Gordon has a connection to the island." She paused for their exclamations of surprise. "Yes, his brother is Jerry Hood, one of the ferry boat captains."

"I know Jerry," Reese said. "He's a good guy. I think he takes fishing and excursion charters out too, on his own boat."

Kaylee thought she knew which captain was Jerry and, now that she thought of it, he looked a little like Gordon: tall and lean, with an intense gaze. "I have to go to Seattle soon. Maybe I can find Jerry and talk to him."

"Good thinking," Jessica agreed.

Mary continued. "Gordon started out as an extra in films about thirty years ago. He was cast in several of Bernard's films as well as others. Gradually he worked his way up to starring roles and then began directing." She held up a picture of a young Gordon and Amy. "He married Amy about twenty years ago. Her career never really got off the ground, but she did write a few scripts with Gordon."

"She was really pretty," Jessica said, studying a photograph of Amy, showing the former actress with feathered bangs and flowing wavy locks. "I wonder why she never became a star."

"It's that elusive thing, charisma," DeeDee said. "Not everyone has it. And you have to be in the right place at the right time too." When everyone stared at her in surprise, she said, "So I'm a closet fangirl. So what?"

"When did Amy and Gordon get divorced?" Kaylee asked.

Mary studied her notes. "It was first mentioned eleven years ago."

The year before Audrey died. Was Amy working for Bernard at that time? Kaylee hadn't seen her name in the articles about Audrey's death, but she could do more digging.

"Something else interesting," Mary said. "I found a connection between Randall and Gordon," Mary said. "They were opening a restaurant together called Randall's."

Kaylee remembered the windbreakers. "Both Gordon and Randall have jackets with *Randall's* stitched on them. I wonder what the status of the restaurant is."

DeeDee snatched up her phone and scrolled. "According to the website, it's closed."

"So that's another thing that might have gone wrong." Kaylee drew a grid on a blank piece of paper. "I'm going to make a chart showing how, when, and where all these people intersected." She'd done similar work when researching and classifying plants.

"Good idea," Jessica said. "I've got a doozy." She clapped a hand over her mouth. "Sorry, Mary. I didn't mean to interrupt."

The older woman smiled at her impulsive friend. "I'm done. Go ahead."

"Okay. First of all, Blair and Randall used to date, and according to the tabloids, they were very serious. It's not clear what broke them up." She looked to Reese.

He shrugged. "Beats me, although my sister might know."

"Well, now Tanya and Randall are dating, according to the tabloids, although when you see them together in person, they don't seem all that close." That confirmed what Kaylee had thought too.

Jessica continued. "But the potentially big news I found is that Gordon and Tanya were enemies." She paused to let that sink in, then held up a newspaper article. "They had huge fights on the set of their last picture together. He was directing and she had a leading role." She passed the article to Reese, who was next to her.

Reese checked the date. "This all happened only a few months ago."

Jessica nodded. "Yes, they only barely wrapped up the film. It won't be released until next year."

"Now you sound like an expert," Kaylee teased. The article came to her, and she scanned it quickly. The insults traded by Gordon and Tanya had been reported by someone unnamed but "close to the set," and they were vicious. Especially the one attributed to Gordon, that Tanya had the talent and "svelte limbs" of a wooden cow.

Had this enmity run deep enough to spill over into murder?

9

Mary was already at the shop the next morning when Kaylee let herself in. "Good morning," Kaylee said. "I feel like I've been away for weeks." She set her to-go cup from the bakery on the counter and gazed around, enjoying the sights and fragrances of her lovely little shop. "I see you've started on the fall window displays. They're cute."

Mary had decorated slim tree branches with colorful silk leaves. A heap of them lay on the floor below, a couple of small teddy bears sitting in them as though playing. They had used the bears in arrangements before, usually with seasonal dress. These bears wore tiny mufflers and hats.

Bear liked the design too. He jumped into the window and grabbed one of the bears in his teeth. Then he trotted over to Kaylee and dropped it at her feet.

Both women laughed. "He thinks he's a hunter," Kaylee said, scooping the bear off the floor. She set it back in the window. "Bear, leave it."

Bear flopped down on his haunches and scratched his ear with his back leg.

"What's on the agenda for today?" Mary asked. She picked up the clipboard with the order list. "I've got arrangements for birthdays, anniversaries, and hospital visits, but nothing too major."

"I'm glad," Kaylee said, pulling her sketchbook out of her tote. At Mary's questioning look she added, "Because otherwise I'd feel terribly guilty about leaving all the work on your shoulders again." She flipped the book open to the set design sketches.

"What do you have there?" Mary sidled closer, adjusting her glasses.

"These are designs for the film. Want to hear about them?" Kaylee hopped onto a stool and picked up her coffee.

Mary set aside the clipboard. "I sure do. Take it from the top."

Kaylee went over the designs, growing even more excited as she described the elaborate arrangements and set pieces. She used photos she'd stored on her phone to illustrate the flowers she was going to use.

"These are gorgeous," Mary said. "All those orchids—" Her eyes lit up. "I just had the most fabulous idea. Why don't we do these on a small scale and sell them as bouquets? We can call them the *Flowers in the Sea* collection."

"I love it." Kaylee's wheels started turning. "I'll make sure Bernard is okay with us using the film name. And he'll probably have us wait until the film is released."

"Of course. But I'm getting other ideas too, for a forest collection. I adore the ferns and astilbe and lilies. We could make living arrangements."

"You're right. Let's come up with some others. They'd be nice indoor gardens over the winter, and then people can plant them outside."

The pair worked on designs for a few minutes, jotting down notes while the ideas were flowing. Kaylee especially loved the combination of lily of the valley, moss, and violet Mary suggested for a dish garden.

But she finally set down her pen. "This has been fun, but I guess I'd better get back to working on the film project. I'm putting together tools and supplies here today and calling in an order to Seattle for tomorrow."

"Are you going over on the ferry?" Mary glanced at the clipboard then selected a vase from the shelf. "You'd said something about that."

Kaylee began to fill in the order form she would e-mail over. "I think so. I want to make sure the flowers are pristine before I buy them. Not that they don't do a good job, but I don't want the delay of a reorder."

"Remember how I mentioned Jerry Hood, the ferry captain, last night?" Mary inserted a piece of florist foam into the vase.

"Gordon's brother. I'd love to talk to him." Kaylee opened a browser on the store computer to check the inventory at the wholesale market.

Mary opened the cooler and selected a few stems. "I wonder which shift he works." She placed an armload of flowers and greenery on the worktable, then reached for the store phone. After a short call, she hung up. "You're in luck. He's running the ferry tomorrow."

Kaylee spun around on the stool and regarded Mary with amazement. "How did you manage to find that out?"

The floral designer's shrug was modest as she handed Kaylee a list of the runs Jerry was working. "I'm a retired police dispatcher, remember?" She winked. "It pays to have connections."

"I'll say," Kaylee said. "And it pays to have friends who have connections."

After lunch, Kaylee returned to the compound. For the first time, the gate was closed and a couple of men she didn't recognize were waiting on the other side in an SUV. Theirs wasn't the only vehicle in the vicinity. She had spotted others parked along the road, men and women pretending to be taking in the views. One man even held a fishing pole.

But she'd seen their cameras and laptops. They were all

reporters, hoping to grab a picture or story they could sell. Her car, identified by The Flower Patch bumper sticker, didn't interest them in the slightest.

She stopped at the gate and unrolled the window. Then she waved her hand and called, "Kaylee Bleu. The Flower Patch."

One man checked a clipboard. After he nodded, the other pressed a button and opened the gate just wide enough for her to drive through. She called a thank-you and hit the gas.

She parked near the house, beside Reese's truck. She had climbed out and was gathering her belongings when he came trotting down the front steps, carrying coiled electrical cords over his shoulder. "You're just in time," he said. "We're filming scenes in the woods." He noticed her slicker in the back seat. "And you'd better wear that."

"Why?" she asked. "It's totally clear today."

"Just trust me."

Reese waited while Kaylee took his advice and put on the bright-yellow garment, feeling quite foolish under the cloudless sky. She left Bear at the house, not wanting him to get wet, and then she and Reese walked out to the film site.

The team was gathered in the woods near where Kaylee had run into Randall after finding Gordon's body. She would never forget that spot, the way the path made several curves right there, evergreens looming overhead.

"All right, everyone," Bernard called. He wore a raincoat too—as did everyone except Blair and Randall—and leaned on his cane. "Let's give the system a quick test."

Reese called out, "Water test. Three, two, one." He turned a valve and water shot out from the slender poles placed along the path, hidden behind trees. The first drops were a light mist, then as he turned up the equipment, they became a driving rain.

"All right, cut," Bernard called. "We're going to start with the lightest rain for the first scene. Blair, you're going to come running around the corner, and at first we'll think you're in danger."

"But she is," Randall said, slinging an arm around Blair and pulling her close. He grinned. "From me."

Shane whistled, and Bernard said, "Save it for the shot, big guy."

Tanya, standing nearby, grunted and folded her arms. Kaylee wondered how it felt to watch the man you were involved with acting romantic with someone else, even if it was his job. But Blair and Randall had once been an item, a hot and heavy one too. The Petal Pushers had nailed that fact down last night in their research. There had even been talk of marriage. Now Blair was engaged to Bernard and Randall was dating Tanya.

"Shane," Bernard said. "Focus tightly on Blair while she's running. Start with her feet. Then her face when she glances over her shoulder." He blocked out the rest of the scene with the two actors and then the shooting began.

Blair ran, looked, and then allowed Randall to catch her. In the shadow of a fir, he kissed her. Both actors were drenched, but they were still beautiful, even with their hair soaking wet and dirt streaking their bare legs.

"That's a wrap," Bernard called and the actors broke apart, trudging toward everyone else on the now-muddy path. Overhead, the sun still shone and birds sang.

Kaylee turned to go, but Reese said, "They're not done. One more scene."

This time the water was turned up to high and the droplets were large and drenching. Blair, in a dry duplicate of the same outfit, was alone on the trail, running. This time real fear shone on her face. The last shot of the scene was a cut to Mervin, who stood wide-legged, one hand holding a machete.

Despite witnessing the mechanics of filmmaking, Kaylee could imagine how this scene would shock the viewers. According to the script, the second running scene would then lead to flashbacks filling in what had happened the day before. Until then, Mervin's role had been that of friendly, harmless groundskeeper.

Kaylee had the feeling that in their real-life case, such a disconcerting surprise might also be waiting.

Once the shooting wrapped, Kaylee retrieved Bear and went back to the greenhouses. She wanted to tag the orchids that she would use in the film to make it easier to grab the right ones. Later, she'd have Reese help her set them up in the great room, where several scenes would be shot.

She was in the far back when she heard whistling and the crunch of footsteps on gravel. To her surprise, Randall entered the greenhouse and stood, hands on hips, to survey the plants. He had changed into jeans, T-shirt, and jacket, but his hair was still damp from filming under the faux rain.

"Can I help you?" she asked, moving into view.

The actor ran a hand over his head and rubbed the back of his neck. "Oh, hi. I didn't know anyone was in here." He glanced around, not making eye contact. "I thought I might, um, hang out in here for a while."

"You're welcome to," Kaylee said. "I'm almost done marking plants for shooting later in the week."

He toed at the gravel underfoot, kicking up a stone. Bear leaped at it. "Yeah. Maybe." He lifted his shoulders briefly. "I didn't want to hang around for the press conference."

Kaylee pressed a piece of orange tape on another pot. "The one announcing the engagement?" According to Reese, they were planning to broadcast live from the house. Jocko McGee was on hand to take photographs and write up an official press release. A case of keeping your enemies close? She'd wondered that when she heard he was coming. It probably wouldn't be the first time a reporter had been bribed to keep quiet. To someone like Jocko, inside scoops about star life were like gold.

"That's the one." Randall's tone sounded determinedly cheerful to Kaylee's ears. "It's not like they want to see the ex hovering in the background."

"I don't know about that." Kaylee studied the pots she'd tagged and decided she had better mark a few more. "Wouldn't it make the story more interesting if you gave your blessing?"

He snorted. "You're almost as cynical as I am. Or perhaps more honest." He stepped closer. "What's that they say? Live by the sword, die by the sword? Using the press to build buzz can be a really slippery slope. They love to watch you on the way down too."

"I thought your career was on the upswing," Kaylee said. "This film is a sure award winner."

Randall bent to examine one of the flowers, cupping a blossom gently with his fingers. "Nothing's ever sure in this business. The script is wonderful, and we've got a great team. The question is, can we all hold it together until the thing's in the can?" For the first time, his eyes met Kaylee's gaze. "Gordon's death has me pretty spooked. If I didn't have an ironclad contract, I'd be out of here."

Kaylee inhaled, weighing out whether to strain their fragile rapport with questions. "About that." She hesitated, then took the plunge. "Who had reason to harm him?"

Anger distorted the actor's handsome features. "Don't get me wrong. Gordon was a great director. And a good scriptwriter too. But he would stab you in the back soon as look at you. He cared about only one thing: Gordon." With each vehement word, he'd stepped closer to Kaylee. Bear growled, and she knew that with one word from her, he would attack. Despite his small stature, the dog had an enormous, brave heart.

"Kaylee?" Reese's familiar voice echoed in the greenhouse.

The actor's head lifted and the anger drained away. "That's my cue," he said. He whirled around and practically ran out of the enclosure, brushing past Reese in the doorway.

Kaylee sagged forward with relief, leaning on a wooden table with both hands. Talk about a miscalculation. She wouldn't broach the topic of Gordon's death while alone with someone ever again.

"What was all that about?" Reese asked. "Are you okay?"

Kaylee lifted her head and attempted to smile. "I'm fine. I made a huge blunder asking him about Gordon. There was no love lost there, to put it mildly."

"Please be careful. There's a killer running around loose and until we know who it is, assume the worst of everyone."

"You're right." Kaylee pointed at the flowers, changing the subject. "I've marked all the plants for the set. Will you help me move them inside later?"

"Sure," Reese said. "I saw a lawn tractor with cart in the garage. We can use them."

Kaylee called for Bear, who came bounding over. "I'm all done here," she told Reese. "Want to go back to the house?"

He assented, falling into step behind her as they emerged from the greenhouses into the late afternoon sunlight. The day was still, and the soft sound of waves on the shore drifted their way.

Next to a hedge a short distance away, Kaylee spotted Randall and Tanya. Whatever they were talking about, it wasn't friendly. He apparently wanted to go in one direction, while she seemed to want him to do something else. Finally she put her arm through his and tugged. Randall gave up and went along.

"What's that all about, I wonder?" Kaylee asked.

"Let's go find out," Reese said. He detoured in that direction and they followed the couple to the formal gardens.

Jocko was photographing Bernard and Blair, who were

standing under an arbor. The first thing Kaylee noticed was Blair's dark-red lipstick, heavy eye makeup, and teased hairstyle. *Exactly like Lily used to wear.* At least in all the pictures Kaylee had seen.

The young actress clung to her future husband's arm as the duo smiled and posed under Jocko's direction. When they moved slightly, she spotted a modern sculpture behind them. They were re-creating the photograph Kaylee had seen in Bernard's office.

She supposed it was a good spot, and maybe there was nothing more to it, but the whole thing was giving her the creeps. Was Blair making herself over in Lily's image? Or was Bernard steering her that way?

Reese watched his cousin with folded arms, his expression stony. Kaylee couldn't blame him.

Jocko lowered the camera. "I think we're good." He caught sight of Kaylee and gave her a terse nod, his gaze uneasy. She waved. As long as the reporter behaved himself, he had nothing to fear from her.

"I want a group shot with the actors," Bernard called, waving them over.

The group posed for several shots, clowning and laughing and making fun of each other. If she hadn't seen the drama and discord for herself, Kaylee would never have imagined it from these publicity stills.

But the masks soon dropped after they dispersed. Kaylee was on her way to talk to Bernard when she heard Tanya whisper to Blair, "You'd better watch out. Bernard already lost two wives. Are you sure you want to go through with this?"

10

Uncertainty and fear clouded Blair's eyes. "Why are you saying this to me? You have Randall now. Can't you be happy for me?"

Tanya was undeterred by this plea. She grabbed Blair's arm. Her eyes glinted as she said in a harsh whisper, "This has nothing to do with Randall." She bit off each word. "You and Bernard. Not a good idea."

The other woman reared back, a tide of red flushing her pale skin. "Are you threatening me?"

Kaylee wondered the same thing. Did Tanya resent Blair taking her friend's place? Or was she afraid Blair would suffer the same fate?

"Of course not," Tanya snapped. "Consider it a friendly warning."

"Don't waste your breath." Blair thrust her chin forward. "I'm going to marry Bernard and there is nothing you can do about it."

"Suit yourself. It's your funeral." Tanya turned and strode off, waving at Randall, who was chatting with Bernard. The actor put an arm around Tanya and drew her close, then gave her a peck on the lips.

Blair's face creased with what looked like pain.

"Are you okay?" Kaylee asked.

"I have a splitting headache. It just came on." The actress swayed on her feet. "I'd better get back to the house and rest."

Reese approached, worry on his face. "What's wrong, Blair?" He had been talking to Shane a distance away.

"Nothing. I don't feel well, that's all." Blair began walking toward the house. Reese and Kaylee joined her.

"I know the engagement is public knowledge now," Reese said. "But you don't have to go through with it. It's okay to have second thoughts."

Blair's penciled brows rose in brown arcs. "You mean second thoughts about marrying Bernard? Sorry, but I'm a girl of my word."

Reese dropped his gaze, not saying anything for a few minutes. "How long have I known you, Blair?" he asked.

She laughed. "All my life, silly. You're older than me."

"That's right." Reese kept his gaze on the gardens. "And have I ever steered you wrong?"

His cousin cocked her head. "Seriously, Reese? I know what you're doing. This is the biggest opportunity I've ever had and I'm not blowing it." She struck a pose. "No more lame ads for car dealerships on local television channels for this girl. Next year I'll be at the Academy Awards, walking down the red carpet." She patted her chest. "Everyone will be looking at me. *Me.* Blair Holt-Martin."

"I can see why that would be attractive." Her cousin studied her with concerned eyes. "If you weren't making such a serious commitment, I wouldn't say anything."

The gloating joy vanished from Blair's face and her features contorted in a scowl. "Why is everyone trying to discourage me? It's my life and I'll do what I want. Butt out." Headache seemingly forgotten, she stormed off, heels clicking on the slate path.

"Boy, I sure blew that," Reese said as they watched her go. "I should have known better from dealing with my sister when she got stubborn. She wouldn't listen either."

Kaylee put a comforting hand on his arm. "Normally I'd say you have to let people make their own mistakes. But let's keep working on her to change her mind—subtly."

Shane whistled and waved at Reese. "That's my cue," the

handyman said. "We have to finish some wiring for tomorrow's shooting."

"I'll see you later," Kaylee said. "Just to let you know, I'm going to the mainland early in the morning, and I'll be gone all day getting other flowers for the movie. Will you help me move the flowers once I get back the following morning?"

Reese gave her a salute. "You bet. Let me know when you need me."

Kaylee and Bear were on the way to the cabin when Jocko McGee hailed her. She stopped to wait for him to catch up, reminding herself to not say anything she didn't want to see in print, such as the sheriff finding the headband or Randall's outburst against Gordon.

"How's it going?" Jocko asked. "I haven't seen you since, you know, that day."

"I'm okay. How are you?" Kaylee flipped the conversation around, determined not to let this become an interview. Well, not his anyway.

Jocko wrinkled his nose and sighed. "It's been rough. Bad dreams." He tilted his head back and studied the sky, where seagulls were circling. "But if I want to get out of fluff reporting, I'd better toughen up."

That was revealing. While he was in a talkative mood, Kaylee asked, "Did you get anything of interest on film that day?"

His eyes lit up. "Yeah, I did. Or at least that deputy thought so."

"Deputy Durham, you mean?" Bear tugged at the leash, so Kaylee began walking again.

Jocko fell into step with her. "That's right. Nick. I didn't catch the killer on film, but he seemed very interested anyway. For a while there, that beach was like Grand Central Station."

"You mean when the police got there?"

"No, before the body was found. Everyone was out there.

Tanya, Blair, Randall, Shane. Even that funny-looking guy, Mervin."

No mention of Bernard. What, if anything, did that mean?

"I'm sure the deputy found those photos helpful." Kaylee hadn't talked to everyone, but she knew that Tanya and Blair had denied being on the beach. Her heart sank at hearing of additional evidence pointing to Reese's cousin.

"So." Jocko lowered his voice. "You got anything for me?"

Kaylee bit her tongue. Then she thought of a countermove. "Are you writing about Gordon's murder?" she asked. "I don't think Bernard will give you any more scoops if you do."

The reporter grunted. "I had to sign a nondisclosure agreement saying I wouldn't. So I'm still stuck with the fluff. But I'm curious, you know?"

Me too. "Hopefully they'll make an arrest soon."

"Yeah. It must be tough working at a house where there have been so many murders." His tone was confidential.

Kaylee burst into laughter. "You don't give up easily, do you?"

"Nope. No one has ever called Jocko McGee a quitter. I keep my eyes on the prize. And sometimes you've got to let the little fishies go if you want to catch the big ones." With that cryptic remark, the reporter took off, muttering that he had to file his story before the deadline.

Kaylee watched him lope away, wondering about the prize story he considered bigger than Gordon's murder.

She returned to Hideaway and got herself organized for the trip to Seattle the next morning. She packed her travel tote bag with things she might need, including treats for Bear and the romance book she'd been reading so she'd have something to do on the ferry. She knew if she didn't bring one, she'd wish she had.

Jessica had stayed in Turtle Cove, so Kaylee decided to go see if Amy needed help with dinner. She wasn't being paid to cook or serve, but she didn't mind helping the assistant, who basically kept the place running single-handed. She gave Bear his dinner and left him at the cabin.

The kitchen was deserted, all the lights off. "Amy?" Kaylee called. She knew she wasn't there, but she checked the pantry and adjacent laundry room anyway.

A faint sound drifted to her ears. *Is that sobbing?* It appeared to be coming from somewhere beyond the laundry room. Amy always entered and left the kitchen from that direction. Her room must be in that wing.

She opened a door, which opened onto a short hallway. The sobbing was louder now. As Kaylee stepped into the hall, a door burst open. Amy, tears streaming down her face, pushed a trash can full of papers through the doorway with her foot.

Kaylee was tempted to slip back into the laundry room, but concern—and curiosity—made her hesitate.

She waited too long, and Amy noticed her.

"Hey, Kaylee." She scrubbed both hands over her face. "I'm a big fat mess, as you can see." She found a tissue in her pocket and blew her nose.

"Is there anything I can do?" Kaylee took a couple of steps down the corridor. "I came over to see if I could help with dinner."

"Really?" Amy cocked her head. "Aren't you the sweetest?" Her voice was hoarse. She cleared her throat and coughed.

"I don't know if I'm that sweet," Kaylee said. "But since Jessica isn't here, I thought you might need the help."

"I'm not cooking dinner tonight. I-I just can't."

Kaylee, sensing a fresh wave of crying building, reached out to pat her hand. "It has been a terrible few days."

Amy gave a sad laugh. "I'll say." Her eyes had a glassy sheen. "I-I hope he didn't suffer. And who killed him? I'm a wreck." She wrung her hands as tears streamed down her cheeks.

"I'm so sorry about Gordon." Kaylee's heart swelled with

sympathy. Even though the couple was long divorced, she clearly still had feelings for the man and was grieving. No one else seemed to understand that. They expected her to carry on as usual.

"I'm sorry about dinner," she whispered, and went back into her room.

Kaylee waited, irresolute. She didn't know Amy well enough to force her company on the woman, and she certainly seemed to want to be alone. But she could do one thing for her, at least. She knocked on the door. "Amy?" No answer, only silence. "I'll take care of dinner."

Kaylee turned around and banged her calf on the trash can. "Ouch." Bending to rub her leg, she glanced at the heap of papers inside.

On the very top was a bound script. In large, bold letters, it read, "*Flowers in the Sea*, a screenplay by Gordon Hood and Amy Early."

Kaylee blinked, not sure she was reading the words correctly. No, they still said the same thing. And meant that Gordon and Amy were responsible for writing Bernard's masterpiece. Since the script had been heaped among obvious trash, she didn't hesitate to grab it, planning to compare it later to the copy she had. What that would tell her, she wasn't certain. But it had to be important. And why would Amy throw it away? Perhaps because it reminded her too much of her dead ex-husband.

Clutching the booklet, she made her escape back to the kitchen. If Amy refused to cook—and who could blame her?—then they could either order takeout from twenty miles away or she could throw something together.

After stowing the script in the bag she was using for the movie, Kaylee tied on an apron then went into the pantry. In the organized cupboard, she quickly found cans of soup. She chose chicken noodle. An index card box caught her eye and she opened it out of curiosity. Her grandmother had kept favorite recipes in one exactly like it.

But instead of recipes, the alphabetized sections held cards with names. She pulled one out at random. "Vegan, low salt, hates beets," it said, under a name she didn't recognize. Amy must use these when planning meals. It was a handy way to log food preferences and dietary needs instead of asking each time someone visited. She quickly glanced through.

Kaylee gathered up the cans and carried them into the kitchen, where she opened them and set a pot to heat. Next she checked the contents of the fridge. She found multiple packages of sliced meat and cheese. Fresh lettuce was in the crisper drawer, and tomatoes and onions sat in baskets on the counter. She'd let people make their own sandwiches. It wouldn't be fancy, but at least they could eat.

Mervin entered the room while she was unwrapping a pound of sliced roast beef. "Where's Amy?"

"She's in her room," Kaylee said, placing the meat on a platter. She reached for the next package, which held sliced Swiss cheese. "She's not feeling well so I'm making dinner. Sort of."

The chauffeur walked across the room and watched her work for a minute. "Sandwiches?"

"Yes. And soup." Kaylee glanced at the man, noticing that his forehead shone with sweat. "Are you feeling okay?" Since arriving at the house, she'd barely exchanged two words with the man. His taciturn nature didn't encourage conversation.

True to form, Mervin didn't answer her question. Instead, he wandered to the refrigerator and pulled out a can of soda. Leaning against the counter, he popped the top and drank.

Despite his silence, Kaylee sensed thick tension in the room. "This project is so much fun to work on. I've come up with some great flower designs." She knew what she was saying was frivolous, even banal, but she wasn't comfortable ignoring him. Besides, maybe he would respond to something.

"Is that so?" Mervin asked. "Glad to hear someone's happy. I wish Bernard had never gone ahead with this project. I told him it was cursed."

Kaylee almost dropped a packet of ham. "Cursed? What do you mean?" Was he talking about Lily's death? Or Gordon's?

Again, he didn't respond. Instead he drained the entire can, crushed it, and tossed it into the recycling bin. Then he stomped out of the kitchen, exiting through the back door.

"All righty then," Kaylee said. She carried platters out to the dining room, along with loaves of bread. Amy had stocked wheat, white, and rye, giving people plenty of choices. Kaylee also set out dishes of mayonnaise, mustard, and relish, as well as a bowl of pickles.

Twenty minutes later, the front doorbell rang. Kaylee waited a minute, but no one went to answer. The bell rang again, this time more insistently. Wiping her hands on her apron, she made her way to the front door.

Deputy Nick Durham stood on the porch. He gave her a tiny nod of greeting. "I have a warrant for the arrest of Mervin Tuttle." He dropped his voice. "His fingerprints were on the murder weapon, a hammer from the garage. The wooden handle was used to strike Mr. Hood."

Stunned, Kaylee put a hand to her chest. "Mervin? Mervin killed Gordon?" She stepped back into the hallway.

Nick walked in, accompanied by two other deputies. "That's what it looks like. Where can we find Mr. Tuttle?"

"He went out the back door," Kaylee said. "I'm not sure where he is."

Bernard trudged up the stairs from his office, using his cane to assist his steps. "Good evening, deputies. How can I be of assistance?"

"We're here to arrest Mervin Tuttle for the murder of Gordon Hood," Nick repeated. He gave Bernard the particulars.

Kaylee's eyes went to Bernard's cane. It had a wooden handle too. But no. There must have been some kind of trace evidence on that hammer, or the police wouldn't make an arrest.

The producer swayed and grabbed the banister to prevent himself from falling. "Mervin? I can't believe it." His face screwed up in puzzlement. "Why, they were the greatest of friends."

"Apparently not," Nick said. "If you don't know his whereabouts, we need to search the property and see if he's here. Do you give us permission?"

Bernard waved a hand. "Yes, of course. I can't believe it." He wandered toward the great room.

Nick conferred with the other deputies. He sent one to Mervin's quarters while he and another left to search the property. "Keep in communication," he told them before he went.

Kaylee went back to the kitchen to check on the soup, which was boiling.

Tanya burst in. "What's going on? There are deputies everywhere."

"They're here to arrest Mervin." Kaylee foraged in the cupboard for a tureen. It wasn't likely that anyone would want to eat, but she went through the motions anyway.

The actress sank down into a chair at the kitchen table and ran a hand through her hair. "So it was Mervin." She spoke in a low voice. "But why? It doesn't make sense."

That's what Bernard had said. "They wouldn't arrest him without evidence," Kaylee said. "The sheriff's department here is very professional."

Tanya didn't answer. Instead she rested her head on her arms, seemingly overwhelmed by the news.

Reese came in through the back door, his face tense. "Kaylee.

Did you hear the news?"

"I did," Kaylee said. "Have they caught up with him yet?"

He shook his head. "No, and they're not likely to. Mervin stole a boat and headed out to sea." He pressed his lips together. "The worst part is, not knowing he was on the run, I helped him launch the boat."

11

A line of cars waited to board the evening ferry, and Kaylee was glad that she'd made a reservation. Although it was off-season, some days were extremely busy, with a lot of traffic back and forth from the islands to the mainland.

The day had gone well from start to finish. Kaylee had been the first one up and about at the compound and left to catch the morning ferry.

After Mervin's flight the previous night, an uneasy atmosphere had descended on the residents of Mukilteo. Their relief at learning who had killed Gordon had been tainted by the uncertainty of the manhunt. A be-on-the-lookout was issued for all of Puget Sound and the mainland coast, including Canada. But with all the isles and inlets in the area, not to mention an entire continent beyond, a man could hide for days, if not weeks. Maybe even years.

Kaylee had gotten all the dahlias, peonies, and greenery she needed at the Seattle wholesale flower market. She'd also found some delphiniums from a local greenhouse and stocked up on those as well. She was glad Bernard had decided to do this version of the movie in color. Now the van was packed with gorgeous, sweet-smelling blooms. She'd put them in The Flower Patch coolers for the night and then take them out to Bernard's in the morning.

Once she parked in the belly of the huge ferry, Kaylee gathered her bag and Bear and headed upstairs. From the railing, she watched the ritual of departure. Men ran around, shouting to each other as they cast off and then guided the craft from its berth. The whistle blew an earsplitting shriek as they got underway, a wake trailing behind.

Kaylee turned her face to the sea breeze, her pulse humming with excitement. Setting off on a journey always thrilled her, no matter the direction. She purchased a coffee from the stand and then found a corner inside to sit with Bear, since the air was too chilly to stay on deck. They watched the shoreline recede and the passengers milling around.

Once the boat was well underway, she decided to try to talk to the captain. She made her way to the wheelhouse, where a mate intercepted her.

"I'm looking for Captain Hood," she said. "I'd like to talk to him for a few minutes once we dock, if he's available." She handed him a folded note explaining who she was and what she wanted.

He regarded her with suspicion. "You're not a reporter, are you? They've been bugging him for days because of his brother's death."

Kaylee found a business card in her pocket and pressed it into his hand. "I'm a florist on Orcas." His mouth opened but before he could speak, she said, "I'm not trying to sell him flowers for the funeral, for heaven's sake. It's personal."

He clamped his mouth shut and took the note. "I suppose you want to wait for an answer?"

Kaylee smiled sweetly. "That'd be good, since you'll never find me again in this crowd."

A couple of minutes later, he was back. "He'll see you once we unload. He'll meet you on the dock." He told her where to wait.

Once the ferry arrived at Orcas, Kaylee drove off and parked next to Jerry's red truck as he'd instructed. Night had fallen, and the headlights of departing cars moved across the pavement and onto the road. Kaylee slumped in her seat with a sigh, eager to get to Wildflower Cottage. But that would have to wait until after she'd talked to Jerry and unloaded at the shop.

Someone rapped on her window, startling her. Captain Jerry

Hood. She unrolled the window. "Thanks for taking time to talk to me," she said. "You must be exhausted."

"You could say that." Jerry's face, so like Gordon's, did look tired. He had bags under his eyes and lines of weariness creased his cheeks and forehead. "I haven't slept a full night since Gordon's death."

"I'm so sorry for your loss," Kaylee said. "It must be hard."

He ducked his head in acknowledgement. "Where would you like to talk?"

An idea popped into Kaylee's mind. "Want to get dinner? We both need to eat, right?" She suggested the Pacific Street Diner, which was near the shop. She'd park the flowers—and Bear—first.

Jerry agreed with her suggestion and they arranged to meet in half an hour. Kaylee drove the familiar streets to downtown Turtle Cove, where she parked behind the shop. From there, she unloaded the buckets of flowers, careful not to bruise the delicate blossoms. She kept some of Bear's favorite food at the shop, so she fed him dinner and filled his water dish. After patting him and promising to return soon, she locked up and left.

The diner was busy at the dinner hour, but Jerry had secured a booth in the back. "I love this place," she said as she slid into the booth.

"Me too," he said with a tired grin. "I always get the flame-grilled cheeseburger and onion rings." He patted his trim midriff. "Makes up for the healthy diet the rest of the week."

"Whatever works." With a laugh, Kaylee pulled the menu from the holder and looked it over. A cheeseburger and onion rings sounded perfect, but she'd go for the junior portion and add mayo, tomato, and lettuce.

The waitress bustled over and they placed their orders, including decaf coffee for Kaylee and regular for Jerry. "I know it won't exactly help me sleep," he said ruefully when Kaylee gave him a questioning glance. "But I just can't make myself drink decaf."

After the server brought their drinks, Jerry asked, "So you were there when . . ." He didn't need to finish.

"I was," Kaylee said, stirring cream into her coffee.

"I'm glad they figured out who did it," Jerry said. "But I heard he skipped town ahead of the deputies."

"He sure did. He stole a motorboat."

Jerry sipped in silence for a long minute. Kaylee didn't press him, figuring it was better to let him lead. "I'm really surprised it was Mervin," he finally said. "The two of them were real tight."

"Mervin and Gordon?" Bernard and Tanya had also said something about the men's friendship.

"Yeah." Jerry's lips twisted in a rueful smile. "If I was a betting man, I would have put money on Randall or Bernard. Gordon wasn't fond of either of them and vice versa."

"I thought Gordon was in business with Randall. Didn't they own a restaurant together?"

Jerry snorted. The waitress approached, platters in hand, and he put up a finger to indicate he would wait to say more when they were alone again. The waitress set down the plates, made sure they had enough ketchup and napkins, then hurried off with a promise to bring coffee refills.

Kaylee's mouth watered when she inhaled the savory aroma of grilled beef and onion rings. She poured a good amount of ketchup onto her plate and dug in.

"As I was saying," Jerry said after chewing his first bite of burger, "that restaurant has already gone under. Gordon was suing Randall for fraud."

"Wow, that's serious." Kaylee thought about that while she took a bite of onion ring. The batter was light and crisp, perfectly fried. "Any business has an element of risk."

"True." Jerry wiped his mouth with a napkin. "But Gordon said he had proof that Randall falsified financial projections and operating records. Gordon had no idea the place was going under or he wouldn't have given him another pile of cash."

So why isn't Randall dead, then? Kaylee's heart thumped.

"You also mentioned Bernard," Kaylee said. "I have to tell you something. I inadvertently heard an argument between Bernard and Gordon." Rather than give details and perhaps steer the conversation, she waited for him to respond.

Jerry waved an onion ring at Kaylee. "You gotta understand. People in show business are just out for themselves. Bernard Martin is a master at that game. I saw it from the get-go, but Gordon could only see what Bernard could do for him."

"They worked together a long time, right?" Kaylee remembered the *Flowers in the Sea* script. How many of Gordon's projects had Bernard taken credit for?

"For about twenty years, at least," Jerry said. "I used to run charters for Bernard and his gang. We'd sail all over these islands for a weekend. I got to see how that man operated up close and personal, you might say."

"So you knew both his wives?" Kaylee realized that this was off the topic of Gordon but she was curious.

"I did. Lovely ladies, both of them." Jerry's eyes were thoughtful. "But like my brother, they had their eye on the main chance. They thought Bernard could do great things for them and, to be fair, he did. Then they both decided to move on."

"And both died." Kaylee set down her burger, sickened.

Jerry sat back in the booth, also abandoning his dinner. "Yes, unfortunately. I always wondered about that. But the sheriff ruled their deaths accidents. Who am I to argue with that?"

The waitress arrived at the table. "Can I get you anything else? Some dessert?"

At their refusals, she slapped a ticket on the table, thanked them, and rushed off.

Jerry grabbed the slip. "My treat." He leaned forward so he could dig his wallet out of his back pocket.

"Are you sure?" Kaylee had planned on buying her own dinner and perhaps his. "But I invited you."

"Not a problem." He set some bills on top of the slip. "It was nice chatting with you. Felt good to get all that off my chest."

"Same here," Kaylee said. She handed him a business card. "Call me if you need to talk some more. I hope I see you again soon." She gathered her belongings.

"You will. I'm usually around, if I'm not running a route."

Outside the diner, Kaylee reflected on their conversation while walking to her car. She'd been glad to get a little more background on Gordon from his brother, although with Mervin squarely in the sheriff's crosshairs, she supposed the mystery was solved. It was interesting that Jerry was also troubled by the untimely deaths of Bernard's wives. *He and Tanya should compare notes.*

"Psst." Kaylee heard a strange sound while she was unlocking her door. Due to the lot being crowded, she'd had to park in the corner by the Dumpster.

She froze and stared around. "Over here," the voice said, somewhere in the trees bordering the lot.

Her heart began to pound. "Leave me alone." She wrenched the door open, prepared to dive in and lock the doors.

"I'm not here to bother you," the voice said. "I just want to tell you something."

"What's that?" Kaylee asked against her better judgment, one leg inside the car.

"It was a mistake." A figure stepped into the glow of a streetlight, just long enough for her to see it was Mervin. Then he melted into the dark.

Kaylee slid into the car and locked the doors, then started the engine. Why on earth had Mervin sought her out and said that to *her*? She fumbled for her phone, knowing she should report the sighting.

Thankfully Nick answered. She told him that she'd seen Mervin Tuttle outside the Pacific Street Diner. She also repeated his cryptic words, to Nick's disdain. "Of course he's going to say that. What criminal doesn't?" They hung up, and as she drove toward the shop to pick up Bear, she heard the wail of sirens.

But she doubted that Mervin would have risked coming out of hiding without a plan to quickly drop out of sight again.

Her phone rang while she was loading Bear into the car. Thinking it might be Nick, she answered without looking. "Kaylee?" a faint female voice said.

"Yes, this is Kaylee."

"Do you know where Reese is?" the woman asked.

Kaylee laughed. That was a new one, someone trying to track Reese down through her. "He's probably at home. Try his cell." She hit the door lock again for good measure, keeping one eye on the shadows, just in case. But the sirens were in the distance now.

"I already did. Three times." Sniffles and tears. "He didn't answer."

She finally realized who it was. "Blair, is that you?"

"Who else would it be?" Another sniff.

Kaylee glanced around again. She needed to get out of here. "Are you okay?"

"No," she wailed. "Someone sent me a threatening e-mail."

12

Kaylee's heart lurched, but she forced calmness into her voice. "Take a few deep breaths, Blair, and then read it to me."

She heard a few gulps, then, "Okay. This is what the e-mail said, 'You're a thief and a cheat, and I'm going to make sure the world knows it. Stay tuned for further instructions.'"

Relief ran through Kaylee like a warm tide. "So they didn't threaten you physically." Though the "further instructions" part was very strange.

"So what?" came the rather sharp reply. "This could ruin my whole life." She softened her tone. "I'm worried it will mess up things with Bernard."

"I'm sure he's no stranger to negative press." That was the understatement of the year. "Maybe you should show it to him. Then the person will be powerless to hurt you."

Blair scoffed. "No way. If you see Reese, tell him I'm looking for him, okay?" She disconnected.

Kaylee set the phone on the seat and put her car into drive. Time to go home and get in bed before something else strange happened. To keep her thoughts off Mukilteo and its denizens, she deliberately thought about flowers the whole way home. She built gorgeous, elaborate arrangements in her imagination, with the result that she was completely relaxed and quite sleepy by the time she pulled into Wildflower Cottage's driveway.

Then her phone rang again. She killed the engine and picked it up. Nick again.

"Tuttle got away," Nick said. "I have no idea how he did it, but there's no sign of him in Turtle Cove or the nearby waters.

Lock your doors and windows. And keep me on speed dial in case he shows up."

Her fatigue fled, replaced by a state of hyper alertness. Could Mervin have followed her home? Would he try to hide out here? She desperately hoped not.

Her night was thankfully undisturbed by unwanted visitors, but Kaylee didn't get a wink of sleep regardless, jumping at small noises and flashes at the corner of her eye. When she swung by the shop the next morning, she was glad to find Mary already there. Her strong arms and energy were welcome as she helped load the buckets of flowers in the back of the van.

"You've chosen some real beauties," Mary said, a dinner-plate dahlia dwarfing her hand as she cupped the huge magenta flower. "They're absolutely stunning."

"I think so too. Today I'm going to build several arrangements for filming." Kaylee hoped she'd be able to get her creative juices flowing. She was exhausted in both body and soul, and the day had barely begun. "I ran into Mervin Tuttle yesterday and ended up staying awake most of the night." As the pair walked back inside the shop, she filled in her assistant about being accosted by the fugitive outside the Pacific Street Diner.

"What a strange thing to risk capture to say to you," Mary said. "What was a mistake? And how on earth does he think you could—or would—help him?"

Kaylee filled a mug with coffee, deciding she had enough time to drink one cup before heading over to Bernard's. "I have no idea. I thought he was long gone by now, either in Canada or on the mainland. He's begging to get caught if he's hanging around Orcas."

"He starred in a lot of action and adventure pictures," Mary said. "Lost in the jungle, shipwrecked, that kind of thing. Maybe he's confused the movies with real life."

"Running away does seem foolish. Even if he is innocent, he's practically confessed."

"Very true," Mary said. "He should turn himself in and get an attorney."

"I'll tell him that next time. Not that I want there to be a next time." Kaylee perched on a stool and glanced through the order book. "You've got a full day here. If you need my help, let me know. I can come back later."

"I'll be fine. But next week we have that wedding, remember?" Mary patted Bear, who had been bugging her for attention. "Think you'll be done by then?"

Kaylee reflected on the shooting schedule. "I should be. Bernard has grouped the shots using flowers together so we'll get those done over the next couple of days to help the flowers stay fresh. Then he can call me back on an as-needed basis." She finished her coffee and carried the mug toward the kitchen area to rinse it. "I'd better hit the road."

Reese's truck was already parked outside the house when she arrived at Mukilteo. She would ask him to help her unload what she'd brought and then move the orchids from the greenhouse into the main house. But before she did that, she was going to check on Blair and maybe see that odd e-mail.

In the great room, Bernard, Shane, and Reese were running wires and setting up tripods and lights for the film shoot. "There's our flower lady," Bernard said. "Ready for your turn to be a star?"

Kaylee forced a smile on her face, hoping she didn't look as wiped out and grumpy as she felt. "I sure am. I have lots of gorgeous flowers waiting out in my van."

"We'll help you bring those in," Reese said. His handsome

features were drawn, as if he hadn't been sleeping well either. "Once we're done here."

"Did Blair get in touch with you last night?" Kaylee asked.

Reese rose from a squatting position behind a piece of equipment, where he'd been plugging in wires. "My phone died yesterday and after I charged it, I saw I had a bunch of missed calls. But when I tried her this morning, it went straight to voice mail."

Bernard chuckled. "That's because she's busy getting beautiful. She doesn't take calls once she's in the middle of makeup." He rubbed his hands together. "One of my rules. You've got to focus if you're going to be good."

Kaylee thought of a concern. "Who's going to replace Mervin?" As far as she knew he'd filmed only one of the many scenes he was to appear in. "Do you have someone in mind?"

"I've got that under control," Bernard said, a bit tersely, as if Kaylee had been questioning his ability to run the shoot. "Another actor will be here at the beginning of the week."

Rather than try to explain or apologize, Kaylee nodded. "I'll get out of your way." She hurried off, heading toward the bedrooms to search out Blair.

This wing of the house had two stories, and Kaylee remembered that Blair's room opened onto the gardens, meaning she was on the lower level. Kaylee passed a staircase leading up and kept going. The carpets were thick, muffling all sound, so when she came around a corner and saw Blair emerging from a doorway, it was hard to say who was more startled.

"Oh. Kaylee. You scared me." Blair closed the door. The actress's face was bare of makeup and her hair pushed back with a headband.

Kaylee's thoughts flashed back to the rhinestone headband the police had found on the beach. This petite woman wouldn't have had the strength to bring down a man of Gordon's size, even from behind. Could she?

"Is that your room?" Kaylee asked. "I thought you were farther down."

Blair shifted one hip, not meeting Kaylee's gaze. "I am. This is Gordon's room. Or rather, it used to be."

Kaylee waited, hoping silence and the pressure of guilt would encourage Blair to talk.

"I left something, um, personal in there awhile ago. But I couldn't get in there until now, since it was sealed." She attempted a laugh. "Obviously I couldn't ask him to give it back."

"Did you find it?" Kaylee's mind buzzed, wondering what Blair was talking about. Could it be the headband? Maybe she didn't know where she'd lost it. Or perhaps it was something else among Gordon's belongings, an item Blair didn't want anyone else to see.

"No. I guess the police took it." Blair bounced on her heels. "I'd better go get ready."

Kaylee remembered her original mission. "Hold on a second. I was hoping to see that e-mail you got. You still have it, right?"

Blair began walking. "I do. Come to my room and I'll show it to you before Amy comes down."

But Amy was already waiting in Blair's room, which was really more of a suite. She gave an exasperated huff upon seeing Blair. "Finally. Where have you been?" Bernard's assistant had set up a mini salon in the bathroom, with a case of makeup and an array of hairstyling implements. The woman's responsibilities and abilities seemed to encompass anything and everything.

"I had an errand." Blair went to a chair and allowed Amy to put a cape around her neck. She darted a glance at Kaylee. "I guess we'll have to talk later."

"That's okay," Kaylee said. "I'd better go start working

on flowers." She hesitated. "I didn't know you do hair and makeup, Amy."

Amy picked up a comb and began to run it through Blair's hair. "I do whatever needs to be done." With expert fingers, she picked up a hot curler and rolled it tight to Blair's scalp, then clipped it. "Gotta make you look cute for your scene with Randall."

Blair's eyebrows knitted in irritation. "Randall is another actor in this movie, nothing more." Her voice was a weary monotone, as if she'd said that before.

Amy rolled another section of hair. "I'm just teasing. But you two were so close. I even heard you were talking about marriage."

"We were, but that's ancient history." Blair reached for a clip and held it up for Amy to take. "And I'm glad it didn't work out. I've finally found Mr. Right."

Despite Blair's bravado, Kaylee heard a hint of doubt. Was Blair trying to convince Amy or herself?

"Mr. Right? His first two wives thought that too."

Blair's mouth dropped open. "You better not let Bernard hear you talking that way. You know they both died in tragic accidents."

Amy looked thoughtful. "I'm sorry I was so blunt. You've got your mind made up, I can see. But just . . . be careful, okay? And if you ever need to talk to someone, I'm here."

Kaylee lingered to see if she'd elaborate, but when nothing else was said, she decided to make herself scarce and get started on the flower arranging.

She took a detour into the kitchen for a cup of coffee. She was filling a mug when she heard a rustling sound in the coatroom near the pantry. There was a door to the outside through that room.

She froze. Judging by the male voices drifting into the kitchen, the others were still in the great room. She also recognized Randall's laugh, so he was with them.

Had Mervin returned? Holding her breath, Kaylee set down her mug and crept quietly across the tiles. The dozen or so steps seemed to take forever. Meanwhile, the rustling was joined by thumps and muttered exclamations.

Kaylee peeked around the corner.

Tanya sat cross-legged on the floor, sifting through a plastic tote of papers. Kaylee recognized it as the one Amy had pushed out of her room. Although Kaylee tried to withdraw as silently as she'd arrived, Tanya glanced up and saw her.

"Hi." Tanya's eyes seemed to challenge Kaylee to question what she was doing.

"Sorry." Kaylee hoped her forced laugh sounded natural. "I thought you were Mervin. I'll leave you to it."

Tanya's eyes grew wide. "Mervin? You think he'd come back here?"

"He's been seen nearby," Kaylee said, not mentioning that she was the one who had encountered the missing man.

"Oh no." Tanya hunched her shoulders and shivered. "He'll probably come looking for me."

"Why is that?" Kaylee asked.

"I told the deputies I saw him going out to the beach that day after I left." She squirmed a little. "They were questioning me too. That reporter took a picture of Gordon and me chatting."

Kaylee leaned against the doorjamb. "What about?"

"Not much." Tanya's cheeks burned red. "He and I didn't exactly get along. He was a jerk. But I thought I should make an effort since we had to work together."

"Sounds reasonable," Kaylee said. *Unless Tanya thought Gordon had something to do with her friend's death and that's what they were discussing.* Kaylee thought of asking Tanya if she'd learned anything new about Lily, but refrained. She really needed to get started on the task she was being paid so handsomely to complete.

Reese and Shane helped Kaylee bring flowers into the house. Bernard had given her the spacious laundry room, where there was a long counter that would serve as a perfect work space. He'd even had a two-door cooler brought in for her.

Reese had built shelves for the orchids, and she arranged the pots and containers on them to create a flower-filled enclave in a corner of the great room. This afternoon, Blair and Randall would film a scene while Blair watered the orchids.

Next, Kaylee went to the laundry room and began to work on arrangements. They would be used that evening for a scene in the great room. She got to work clipping stems and trimming leaves, preparing the dahlias, delphiniums, and peonies for two massive displays. These would be placed on either side of the fireplace.

The sound of a woman's voice drifted into the room. "I told you not to. I know it's hard." *Amy.* It sounded like she was on the phone.

Kaylee tried not to listen. She went to the cooler and grabbed another couple of delphiniums. Some of them were a lighter blue and she liked the contrast with the deep pink dahlias and white peonies.

"Be careful, okay?" Amy said. "What you did was really stupid. You know that, right?"

13

Was Amy talking to Mervin? Some instinct told Kaylee that it was entirely possible. *But that would mean she is aiding and abetting.* Despite her earlier resolution not to snoop, Kaylee paused and tried to listen to Amy.

Footsteps sounded on the tile, coming from the opposite direction. Bernard appeared in the doorway, beaming. "I've just had the best idea, Kaylee."

Amy's voice grew fainter and a few seconds later, a door shut.

"What is it? I can't wait to hear." Kaylee tried to inject enthusiasm into her voice, hoping that he wasn't going to demand new designs from her. And, to be honest, she would have liked to have heard more of Amy's side of that conversation.

Bernard clasped his hands, as though in entreaty. "How would you like to be an extra in the film? I want to add additional people to the evening scene."

Kaylee set down her snips. "Oh no, I can't do that. I'm no actress."

The producer picked up a dahlia and sniffed it, then frowned and set it down. Dahlias didn't have much scent. "It's not a speaking role. I want to find several attractive couples to mingle in the background, as though at a party."

An idea trickled into Kaylee's mind. "How many people do you want? I can ask Jessica and several of my other friends." DeeDee would be beside herself at the chance to be in a movie. "Their husbands might agree too." *They* might have to be dragged kicking and screaming, but Kaylee knew the men would eventually agree.

Bernard smiled. "Would you ask them? You'd all get paid,

of course. Simple evening wear will be fine." He gave her several more details about the shoot and when people needed to arrive to get ready and have their hair and makeup done. Filters would be used so they wouldn't actually be filming at night.

Kaylee pulled her phone out of her pocket. Whom to call first? She settled on Mary. "Hey, lady," she greeted her assistant. "How would you like to be in a movie?"

Mary gasped. "Do you mean it?"

"You and Herb are needed as extras tomorrow." She gave Mary the details. "I also want to see if we can get the other Petals and their husbands to do it too."

"I'm sure they will. Want me to call them?"

"That'd be great. I really should get my work done." Kaylee eyed the urns she was using. The arrangements were going to be so tall and heavy, she'd need a flat dolly to move them. "Call me back and let me know what they say."

A framework of wire and bamboo went into each urn for support. Then she added flowers, building from the bottom up. They would look spectacular on either side of the majestic fireplace in the great room, if she did say so herself.

Kaylee was adding accent foliage when Reese sauntered into the room.

"Wow." He gave a whistle. "I'm impressed." He circled the closest urn, admiring it from every direction.

"Thanks. I've been working on them for hours." Kaylee straightened, a hand on her lower back, which ached. She'd been so absorbed, the afternoon had flown by. She loved it when that happened.

"Guess what?" Reese said. "I'm going to be in the movie." He made a comical face of pride.

"Me too," Kaylee said. "And so are the rest of the Petal Pushers and their hubbies." She'd gotten texts confirming, along with a request for an impromptu meeting at Wildflower Cottage that evening to decide on outfits to wear.

"That should be fun," Reese said. He eyed the arrangements. "Want a hand moving those?"

"Yes, tomorrow. I'll leave them in here overnight. There's less traffic." Out in the main room, they might be subject to damage if someone touched or bumped the flowers. Kaylee began cleaning up the plant and wire scraps and tossing them into a trash can.

"Good idea." Reese lowered his voice. "I've been assigned to change the locks on Mervin's apartment."

"Can I tag along?" She'd welcome the opportunity to look around the fugitive's living space.

Reese smiled. "Why do you think I told you?"

They made their way outside so Reese could gather his tools and two new locksets from his truck.

"Is Bernard worried about Mervin coming back here?" Kaylee asked as they strolled to the garage, where Mervin lived upstairs over the bays. Security personnel were still guarding the gate, joined now by a sheriff's cruiser watching for the fugitive. But since he was traveling by water—unless he'd switched to a car—there were plenty of spots he could enter the property.

"I'm guessing that's it," Reese said. He led the way up a flight of stairs to a hallway. He pointed at a couple of doors. "That's where Shane and I stay. Mervin's apartment is down this way."

They stepped into a living room with a view of the woods in back. The room wasn't large, but it had big windows that let in lots of light. The furnishings were simple, only a sofa, recliner, and a couple of occasional tables. A large television hung on the wall, along with movie posters. A shelf held a line of awards.

"I wonder how he felt ending up here after that." Reese nodded at a poster depicting Mervin in *Jungle Mission*. The actor pushed aside spiky jungle plants with a ferocious glare on his face. He wore a camouflage suit and carried a number of guns.

Kaylee glanced around at the modest apartment, trying to imagine. Mervin hadn't ever been a top star but he'd at least been a headliner in B films. Now he did bit parts and lived above a producer's garage. No, now he was on the run from a murder charge.

While Reese changed out the lock on the front door, Kaylee wandered through the rest of the apartment. The kitchen and bedroom were both remarkably spare, like the living room. Mervin had few belongings or personal items. The kitchen cupboards only held basics, which was understandable since he probably ate most meals over at the house. In the bedroom closet, which stood ajar, Kaylee noticed a navy-blue windbreaker that looked familiar. On impulse, she grabbed the hanger.

As she suspected, it was a Randall's jacket, exactly like the ones Gordon and Randall had. She also found a Randall's ball cap on the top shelf.

She stood in the bedroom for a long moment, studying the items. Maybe Mervin had received them in a promotion, but her intuition said otherwise.

Had the actor been involved with the ill-fated restaurant along with Gordon and Randall?

Reese wandered into the room. "Everything okay in here?" His gaze fell on the clothing. "What's that?"

Kaylee explained its significance. She also realized she hadn't told him about the sighting. "I saw Mervin outside the diner last night." She gave him the details while stowing the clothing back in the closet.

Reese was taken aback. "He's still on Orcas?"

"As of last night. If he's smart, he's long gone now." Yet something told Kaylee Mervin was still lingering nearby.

But why?

"Come on in," Kaylee said to the ladies on her front porch later that evening. She felt a smile stretch across her face at the sight of her three dearest friends.

"I brought lasagna, as I promised," Mary said. She carried a big baking pan, holding it with two oven mitts. "Careful, it's still hot," she cautioned when Kaylee reached for it.

"I have salad." DeeDee held a huge plastic container under one arm.

Jessica was right behind her, holding a bakery bag. "And obviously I have dessert. But we may want to diet for our big debuts."

"We won't lose much in a day," Mary said. "So we might as well use our best foundation garments and go for it." She patted her middle. "Spandex is my secret weapon."

"Speaking of which, where are your outfits?" Kaylee asked. The plan was for them each to try on several possibilities and pick out what they would wear on screen.

Mary turned toward the door. "In the car. I'll go out and get them."

"Me too," DeeDee said. "Jess, give me your keys and I'll grab yours as well." She handed Jessica the salad and accepted her keys.

Balancing the bowl and bag, Jessica followed Kaylee to the kitchen. "This is so exciting. I can't believe we're going to be in a movie." She set down her burdens.

"It is fun." Anticipation bubbled in Kaylee's belly as she pulled her contribution to the meal—garlic bread—out of the oven. She'd never had the slightest desire to be in front of a camera, but now that it was imminent, she might as well enjoy the ride.

DeeDee and Mary brought in several garment bags, and then they set the table. They all sat to eat, passing the food around family style.

"So what do your husbands think about being extras?" Kaylee asked. Mary's lasagna recipe was among the best she'd ever eaten, with bold Italian sausage, creamy ricotta cheese, perfectly cooked noodles, and a robust tomato sauce. It was beautifully seasoned with plenty of garlic, basil, and oregano.

"Andy didn't know what to think," DeeDee said with a laugh. Andy was the manager of an organic grocery store. "But he's pretty outgoing, so I think he'll be fine."

"Herb is into it," Mary said. She reached for the salad bowl and served herself a big scoop. "He can't wait to brag to all his buddies."

Jessica took a bite of cheesy lasagna and chewed. "Yum. Luke went right to the barbershop today for a haircut after he heard the news." Luke was an accountant, who managed to keep up with his bubbly wife. "Now he wants to wear a fedora, even though we'll be inside."

Everyone laughed. "I'm sure he'll look good," Kaylee said. "All the husbands will."

"So what's new with the manhunt?" Mary asked. "I keep hearing about it on the news."

"I'm not sure," Kaylee said. "Mervin hasn't shown up at Bernard's house, at least as far as I know. A cruiser was parked there all day." Kaylee told Jessica and DeeDee about her encounter with Mervin. "The whole thing doesn't make sense," she added. "By all accounts, he was Gordon's friend."

"I think it's time for a little more digging," DeeDee said. "The answer has to be in his background." As the owner of a mystery bookstore, DeeDee considered herself well-versed in investigation techniques. "Maybe visit the library?"

"That's a good idea," Kaylee said. "Now that the arrangements are done, I have time tomorrow morning." The Orcas Island Library had access to databases she wouldn't be able to access on her own.

After finishing dinner, the ladies helped Kaylee clean up. Then they started the mini fashion show. The plan was to try on outfits in Kaylee's bedroom and model them in the living room for the others to judge.

While Mary was getting changed, DeeDee pulled up an article on her phone. "I did some research into what you should and shouldn't wear on camera," she told Kaylee.

"Like what? Stripes and checks together?" Kaylee laughed, imagining herself dressed in unflattering wide horizontal stripes or a loud houndstooth. Not that she ever wore them.

DeeDee nodded. "Exactly. They say to avoid white blouses and clothes in black, yellow, and red, as well as prints and busy geometrics."

"So what should we wear?" Kaylee asked.

"Neutrals, dark blue, jewel tones, browns, that kind of thing," DeeDee said. "We want to be attractive without drawing too much attention from the main action."

Mary strolled out into the living room, smoothing a trim purple top over her hips. She wore it with a silky pair of attractive ivory trousers. Discreet jewelry adorned her ears, neck, and wrists.

"That's it," Jessica said. "Gorgeous and elegant."

"You think?" Mary turned slowly around so they could see all sides.

DeeDee gave her a thumbs-up. "Sold. Jess, you're next."

Jessica slipped into the bedroom and emerged a few minutes later wearing a silk suit in a dark teal. The color flattered her brown hair and eyes. "I bought this for a wedding a couple of years ago." She tugged at the jacket. "I'd be happy to get more use out of it."

"That's perfect too," DeeDee said. "I guess you guys paid attention to me when I sent you that article."

"Of course we did," Mary said, back in her regular clothes.

"You're next, DeeDee," Kaylee said. "I'm still thinking about what to wear." Mentally she was rummaging through her closet, trying and discarding outfits.

"We'll help you," DeeDee promised. She vanished into the bedroom, returning a few minutes later in a sapphire-blue fit-and-flare dress that hit her long legs just at the knee.

"I love it," Jessica said. "That color is perfect with your eyes and hair."

"And flattering to your figure," Mary added. "What I wouldn't give for your legs."

DeeDee checked her reflection in a wall mirror. "They're great until you try to find pants long enough." Her eyes met Kaylee's in the glass. "Your turn."

Kaylee threw open her closet and let the others go through it with her. She really had no idea what to choose. She was so much more comfortable in casual clothing, like jeans and a T-shirt. She rarely wore skirts, even back in her teaching days. After all, botanists spent a lot of time mucking about in fields and gardens.

The three women conferred before DeeDee held up a long dress in hunter green. "This is it," she announced. "Try it on for us."

"Okay." Kaylee regarded it dubiously. "I hope it still fits. I haven't worn it for ages." She'd bought it for a formal faculty dinner years before.

They left the room, and Kaylee tried on the dress. To her relief, it slipped on with ease. She tied the sash around the waist and examined herself in the dresser mirror. Not too bad for her screen debut.

Kathy Fitz's dress would look terrible on camera. Kaylee thought as she walked into the library the next morning and spotted the head librarian wearing a bright red-and-yellow print. Kathy often wore colorful clothing, and she had the height, build, and versatile coloring to pull it off.

The librarian glanced up from her computer and smiled. "Hey, Kaylee. How's it going?" On the counter beside Kathy's elbow was a copy of the tabloid Jocko worked for. *Love Blossoms Amid Tragedy on* Flowers *Set,* blared the headline. Below it was a picture of Blair and Bernard laughing as they strolled on the beach. That was a tasteless choice, considering that was where Gordon had died.

"I didn't know the library subscribed to that particular publication," Kaylee said, pointing at the newspaper.

"We don't." Kathy glanced around at the other patrons—an elderly man in the reading room and a couple of women browsing the shelves—and whispered, "It's mine." In a slightly louder voice she said, "I couldn't resist. It's all happening right here on Orcas."

Kaylee was all too aware of that. "Yes, I know. I'm the flowers part of *Flowers in the Sea.*"

Kathy's mouth made an *O.* "Wow, that must be so exciting. You'll get to see your creations on the big screen."

"And myself." Excitement tingled through her at the admission, and she felt her cheeks heat. "I'm also going to be an extra." She gave Kathy a few details about the scene and the participation of the other Petal Pushers.

The librarian clapped her hands in delight. "Good for you all. I can't wait to see it." She clasped her hands. "We'll do a screening here when the movie comes out on DVD or streaming."

They smiled at each other another moment, then Kaylee said, "I'm here to do some research on the databases."

Kathy nodded wisely but didn't probe. "Come this way and I'll get you set up." The librarian escorted her to a computer station where she helped Kaylee log in. "We're really lucky to have access to these," she said, her fingers flying over the keyboard. "They normally cost thousands."

Kaylee was grateful, since she didn't have the money, time, or contacts for deep background research. Before beginning to dig, she paused to organize her thoughts.

First she'd look for more information on the victim, Gordon Hood. She skipped over mentions of his career moves, having already gotten a good picture earlier with the Petal Pushers. After scanning dozens of articles, she stumbled on a mention of his divorce from Amy, which cited it as "contentious." That wasn't what Amy had said, nor was it the way she'd acted, but the bereaved had a habit of revising history. As did the tabloids. After all, an amicable divorce was not nearly as interesting. With a few clicks, Kaylee found the public record of Gordon and Amy's divorce.

In addition to a house, which Gordon kept by paying Amy a chunk of cash, their largest asset was their body of screenplays. The various scripts had been divided between the couple, with *Flowers in the Sea* given to Gordon. Had Amy thought the project would come to nothing? She'd been granted several that Kaylee recognized, films that had made money at the box office. Amy must have been happy about that, but did she resent being cut out now that Bernard was making this film? Maybe that was why she'd tossed the script. It was a reminder of an earlier poor decision.

But Amy was clearly grieving for Gordon. And she wasn't the one accused of killing her ex-husband. That was Mervin.

The restaurant, Randall's, seemed key to the mystery since it connected Gordon and Randall—and possibly Mervin, based on that jacket and ball cap.

Next Kaylee chose a legal database that logged civil cases and also indexed business articles and filings. A search for Randall's in Los Angeles brought up several documents. The corporate filing didn't reveal much since an attorney was the registered agent.

The legal cases were more revealing. Gordon was suing Randall for "breach of fiduciary duty," a fancy term for what Kaylee guessed was mismanagement of money. It was in the other named parties where she struck gold. Mervin Tuttle was a coplaintiff, also seeking the return of his investment and damages from Randall.

Kaylee studied the screen, both vindicated and puzzled. To all appearances and by all reports, Mervin and Gordon had been friends. They were even jointly suing Randall regarding the ill-fated restaurant venture.

So why would Mervin kill Gordon? Had Gordon wanted to drop the suit? Kaylee continued searching and found no mention of this.

She decided to keep digging, starting with Mervin's background. After a few minutes, she came across something very interesting. Mervin had filed for bankruptcy about ten years before, around the same time his career took a nosedive. For most of the period since, she guessed he'd been working for Bernard. Then he'd scraped together some savings and made an investment, only to have it fail.

That would make someone angry. But at the person who took the money and ran—which would be Randall, right? Unless Gordon had talked him into investing. That was a possibility.

She thought about Randall's. The men had all received the

blue windbreakers, perhaps as a sign of partnership. Something hit her with the certainty of truth. Something she should have realized much earlier.

Two tall men. Identical clothing. Early morning fog.

It was a mistake, Mervin had said.

The wrong man had been killed.

14

Kaylee sat staring at the screen for a long moment, lost in thought. Mervin had meant to kill Randall. And Mervin was still free.

That meant Randall was in danger. Kaylee reached for her cell phone to call Nick, then hesitated. Not in here, where someone might overhear. And what of her research? Her fingers fumbling with urgency, she sent several documents to the printer. She also e-mailed them to herself.

"Find everything you need?" Kathy asked when Kaylee charged up to the counter.

"I think so." Kaylee paid for the copies, accepting the papers and tucking them into her bag. "I hate to run but I've got a lot to do."

Kathy grinned. "Getting ready for your big debut? Good luck. I mean, break a leg." She gave Kaylee a jaunty wave before turning to help a woman check out.

Kaylee bolted for her car, which was warm and private. She slid into the driver's seat and started the engine, then dialed Nick's number. He didn't answer, so she left a message. "Nick, this is Kaylee. Please call me. I've figured out something important about Mervin."

She hated to be so cryptic, but her theory was too involved to leave in a voice mail. A vague claim that Randall was in danger might easily be regarded as too far-fetched. But mentioning Mervin should do the trick.

Nick called when she was on the way to the compound, after stopping by the shop to fetch Bear and check in with Mary. She pulled over onto the wide shoulder of the road.

"Kaylee. You have information for us?" Nick sounded terse but she didn't take offense. The manhunt must be taxing the deputies' nerves as well as their resources.

"Yes. I wouldn't have bothered you, but this seemed too important not to share." She inhaled a breath. "I think the wrong man was killed. I don't think Gordon was the target."

Silence on the other end. "What are you talking about?"

Kaylee explained, telling Nick about the identical clothing and similarities in build and height between the two men. She mentioned again what Mervin had said, which made perfect sense from this angle. Finally she shared the research she'd done at the library.

"So you think Tuttle meant to hit Randall James but mistakenly struck Gordon Hood instead?" He paused as though digesting this. "That's all very interesting but it doesn't really have any bearing on the case. We have evidence that Tuttle killed Gordon and that's what matters."

"I know." Kaylee took another breath. "But until Mervin is in custody, Randall could be in danger." She didn't know for certain that Mervin would try to complete his botched mission, but surely it was a possibility. Was the penalty that much worse for two murders than one? Was murder easier the second time, after the line had been crossed?

Nick released a breath. "We've stationed a cruiser at the property. We're scouring the islands and waters for Tuttle. There's really nothing else we can do."

Bear growled at something and Kaylee studied the woods lining the road. For all she knew, Mervin could be out there, watching her. She shivered. "I hope you find him soon."

The deputy barked a laugh. "You and everyone else. If you get any inkling, any hint that he's on the property, call me immediately, okay? And then inform our people at the gate."

After they exchanged goodbyes, Kaylee set her phone down and pulled onto the road. Regardless of what Nick said, she needed to warn Randall. Tired of her squirrel-cage thoughts, Kaylee turned on the radio. After a few minutes of soothing classical music, a weather forecast came on. An intense storm featuring high winds, heavy rain, and storm surges was predicted to hit Puget Sound within the next twenty-four hours or so.

"As long as it holds off until tomorrow," Kaylee muttered, glancing at the overcast sky. She didn't want her friends to be caught trying to drive home in bad weather.

When she reached the estate, Kaylee was relieved to see the cruiser parked at the gate. The security guards were also on alert, and they took care to check her name, although they'd seen her before. She also gave them a list of the evening's guests, as she'd been instructed.

At the house, Bernard was directing Amy, Reese, and Shane as they prepared the great room for the evening shoot. The furniture was moved around to facilitate filming the scene. Kaylee and the other guests would appear in the background of the main action. Shane and Reese ferried the flower arrangements in from the laundry room and set them up on either side of the fireplace, where Kaylee had envisioned them.

"Bravo," Bernard said, clapping his hands. "Quite spectacular indeed."

Kaylee allowed herself a moment of satisfaction as she admired the vibrant colors of the elaborate arrangements, their shape and scale contrasting nicely with the huge fireplace. It was wonderful to imagine something and bring it to life. No doubt screenwriters felt the same way about film projects.

That thought reminded her of Amy, who was busy making final touches to the furniture grouping. How did the writer feel about being cut out of this project? She seemed okay with it, but was she really?

Perhaps sensing Kaylee's gaze, Amy glanced up and their eyes met. Kaylee, caught off guard, blurted the first thing that came to mind. "Amy, I gave the visitor list for tonight to the security guards. I have another if you need it."

"I don't." Her smile was grim. "As long as they know who to let in—and who to keep out. It's always so difficult trying to keep projects like this from becoming a circus."

Bernard turned from his contemplation of the flowers and the portrait of Lily, which still hung there. "Speaking of which, I've invited Jocko McGee tonight. He's going to take still photographs for us."

Jocko must be over the moon about that. Kaylee had learned that film projects often employed photographers to create images used in publicity and marketing materials.

Amy kneed an ottoman into place. "I'd better let the gate know to add him to the list. They're under strict orders when it comes to the press."

"And escaped felons," Shane stage-whispered to Reese. The cameraman laughed out loud at his own poor joke.

Reese shot him an irritated glance. "If we're all done here, Bernard, I'd like to go get ready." He ran a hand over his rumpled locks and grinned. "I don't want to look like this for my camera debut."

Before she could stop the thought, Kaylee mused that she couldn't see anything wrong with his looks at the moment.

Bernard pivoted where he stood, regarding every inch of the room. "I think we're all set. Camera call is at six." As Shane started to walk off too, Bernard called him back. "Hold on, Shane. Let's check the shooting angles one more time."

Shoulders slumped, Shane stomped over to one of the cameras

already set on a tripod. He peered at the screen while Bernard issued commands.

Kaylee also made her escape, feeling an urgency to warn Randall. He and Tanya liked to use the gym on the lower level, so she thought she'd start there.

She was in luck. The actor was alone, trotting on the treadmill while watching television. On the screen was a visual of the approaching storm, which looked like it would engulf all of the San Juan Islands.

Randall noticed her in the mirrored wall and gave a friendly wave. "I'll be done soon," he called. The treadmill speeded up and his muscular legs flashed faster, arms pumping. He panted in time with his pounding feet.

Kaylee walked closer so he could hear. "I actually need to talk to you. It's really important."

He threw her another glance, this one confused. He checked the display. "Okay. Give me five."

She nodded and exited the room to give him privacy while he finished his workout. Leaning against the wall outside, she tried to frame the discussion ahead. She still hadn't decided on an approach to the topic when he emerged from the gym, scrubbing at his sweaty head with a towel.

"Hey." He slung the towel around his neck. "What's up?" He gestured down the hall. "Want to talk on the way to my room?"

"Let's stay here," Kaylee said. "I don't want anyone else to hear this."

Randall narrowed his eyes. "That sounds ominous." But he complied, shifting his weight into a more comfortable stance.

Kaylee inhaled. "It kind of is." She swallowed. "I think you were Mervin's intended victim, not Gordon."

He jerked his head back. "What? Why would you think that?"

She ticked off the reasons. "Because you and Gordon wore

the same windbreaker. You're both tall and lanky." She hesitated then plunged ahead. "And Mervin was suing you, not Gordon."

Randall's lip lifted in a snarl. "You're well-informed, aren't you? You always dig into your clients' private lives?"

The sudden attack knocked Kaylee off-balance, but only for a moment. "You're not my client. Bernard is." She rested her hands on her hips, her temper rising. "I'm only trying to help you. But I don't have to. Good luck." She turned to go, eager to put distance between herself and the actor.

"Kaylee," he called. "Wait."

She stopped, but didn't turn around.

"I'm sorry," he said, coming alongside her. He played with the towel, sawing it back and forth behind his neck. "The lawsuit . . . it's a sore subject." He sighed. "Not that I'm making excuses, but I was acting under bad advice."

Kaylee didn't know if he was telling the truth, nor did she really care. He would have to live with the results of his business dealings and whatever decisions a judge made regarding them.

"You don't need to explain to me," she said. "I just couldn't figure out why Mervin would kill Gordon since everyone has told me they were good friends. And when I saw you that morning, wearing almost identical clothing, it struck me how much you resembled Gordon at first."

Randall, still clasping both ends of the towel, studied the carpet. "So you think he made a mistake? Gordon was hit from behind, I heard. If his hood was up, I could see how that happened." Wincing, he shook his head as though trying to dislodge the image. "I like to sit in that same spot. I can't believe I never put it together."

His remark about the beach further confirmed Kaylee's theory. Mervin must have seen Randall there on more than one occasion.

The actor glanced at Kaylee with a haunted expression. "I sure hope they catch him soon."

The ladies got ready for the shoot at Kaylee's cabin while the husbands joined Reese in the main house, in a makeshift dressing room.

"This place is so cute," DeeDee said. "No wonder you wanted to stay on-site." She and the others had climbed the stairs into the sleeping loft. "There's a great view of the water from up here."

"It's one of my favorite features." Kaylee joined her at the large window overlooking the bay. She noticed the heavy clouds and the racing waves edged with whitecaps. "I sure hope the storm holds off until after you all get home."

"Me too." Mary peeked over Kaylee's shoulder. "Let's take our regular clothes up to the house so we can leave from there, in case it starts raining."

"Sounds like a plan," Jessica said. She turned toward the stairs. "Let's get started. I think the curling iron is ready."

The hour spent getting ready with her friends, laughing and joking as they put on makeup and fixed each other's hair, was a respite for Kaylee. *An oasis of normalcy,* she thought. Her worries about Mervin, Gordon's murder, and concern for Blair's well-being all fell away.

After they were ready, they put on coats and trudged to the main house, carrying their dress shoes. Overhead, the wind whipped through the trees, rustling the leaves and making the fir boughs sway. A muffled booming came from the waves pounding the shore.

"Good thing I used lots of hair spray," Mary called. She began to run, and with shouts of laughter the others did too.

Kaylee led them through the back entrance and into the great room. The husbands and Reese stood huddled together near one of the windows, handsome in their dress shirts, sport coats, and slacks. They reminded Kaylee of attendants at a wedding, waiting for the bride.

In unison, the men turned and beamed at their women, including Reese, whose eyes lit with admiration. Kaylee had rarely seen the carpenter in anything but his trademark flannel shirt and jeans. He cleaned up nicely.

Amy bustled up. "Let me fix your hair, okay?" She brushed Kaylee's disheveled locks back, clucking. "Sit at the dining table." She ushered the women in that direction.

"We should have gotten ready here," Kaylee said with a laugh. "It's getting really windy." Outside the big picture windows, the trees shivered and bowed. Wind howled down the chimney.

"Is this going to affect filming, boss?" Shane asked.

Bernard rubbed his chin, considering the set and the actors. "No. It will only add a touch of the eerie. I say we roll and see what we get."

Jocko McGee arrived, and he and Bernard discussed the shots he would take, before, during, and after shooting.

Amy fussed over each of them, doing touch-ups and adding even more hair spray. Trying not to breathe in the noxious fumes, Kaylee was thankful she rarely bothered with the stuff. She preferred to let her hair do its own thing.

"Your makeup is in good shape," Amy said. "It needs to be laid on pretty thick or else you'll be washed out on camera, and it looks like someone knew that." She checked each face, which sported red lips and cheeks and plenty of eyeliner, shadow, and mascara.

DeeDee smiled. "Thanks. I've done a lot of amateur theatricals, and I read up on what to do for film."

Amy gave a nod of approval.

After they were primped to Amy's satisfaction, Bernard placed them in their spots and explained what to do. They were to engage naturally in conversation while pretending to sip drinks. Platters of canapés were placed on the table, but they weren't required to actually eat them.

"You might find it interesting when we're focused on the main actors, but you have to ignore them," Bernard said. "We can't have you all staring at the action. Although when Blair tosses a drink at Randall, we'll have you react to that."

"How will we know when it's coming?" Luke asked, his brow furrowed in concern. Jessica's husband had been taking everything in with the laser attention he brought to his accounting work.

"We'll do a separate take for that." Bernard grinned. "Keep your fingers crossed we get it in one. Otherwise Randall will be changing clothes."

"Poor guy," Andy said with an affable chuckle. "It's bad enough having that happen once."

DeeDee, beside him on the couch, gave him an elbow. "Like you'd know. Besides, it's only a movie."

"True, but we need you to forget that." Bernard waved his hands, indicating the set. "You are guests at a very fine home, but you're not immune to the dangerous undercurrents among those who live here. During that scene, you will all watch as Randall approaches Blair. He's not supposed to be in here, so you know a confrontation is brewing."

"Why does she toss water at him?" Jessica asked. "I thought she loved him."

Bernard wagged a finger at Jessica. "You're right. She does. But she doesn't want her husband to know that. She's trying to hide it with an angry action." He glanced over his shoulder at Blair, Randall, and Tanya, who were strolling into the room.

"We're going to get started. Thanks again, all."

"Thank you," Herb called. To the others, he said, "I can't wait to tell the grandkids their boring old gramps is in a movie."

Mary straightened his shirt collar. "You're not boring, dear. Just excitement challenged."

Everyone laughed, and then watched while Bernard set up the scene, placing the main actors in their spots. Soon Bernard called, "Lights, camera, action!" and filming began.

Bernard and Blair had an intense scene, followed by Blair throwing the water at Randall. Tanya meanwhile, in her role as housekeeper, hovered and glared. Her hatred for the others was quite believable.

A couple of hours later, Bernard declared it a wrap. Relieved from their duties, cast and crew surged from their spots, chattering and laughing.

"We've got real refreshments in the dining room," Amy said. The throng headed that way, eager to quench thirst and nibble.

The doorbell rang. Kaylee, who was lagging behind, went to answer since no one else seemed to notice in the hubbub.

Nick stood on the porch, rain dripping off his cap. She glanced past him into the night. The storm had arrived. Rain was sheeting down, the cruiser with its whirling lights barely visible.

"Kaylee, is Mr. Martin here?" Nick's voice sounded strained.

She opened the door wider. "Yes. We just finished filming."

Nick brushed past her. "I'll wait here. I'm soaking wet."

Kaylee started across the floor then halted. "What's happened, Nick?" She knew the deputy well enough to guess it wasn't a routine call.

He'd taken his hat off and held it with one hand while running the other through his wet hair. "It's Mervin Tuttle. We've found his boat offshore, drifting and empty."

15

Kaylee froze, unable to move forward. Slowly she circled to face the deputy. "You found the boat, but without Mervin?"

Nick was clearly miserable. "That's about the size of it. He must have gone overboard. The wind and waves are terrible right now. There's a small craft advisory already posted."

Jocko shambled into the foyer, humming. He saw the deputy and stopped dead, stiffening in a fashion that reminded Kaylee of a bird dog. "Deputy. What's up?" He was already fumbling for his phone.

"I'll go get Bernard," Kaylee told Nick quietly. She continued into the main part of the house. A quick glance around the great room revealed that Bernard wasn't there. People were gathered around the dining room table, eating and laughing. The Petal Pushers and their significant others appeared to be on cloud nine, still elated from their successful camera debut.

Voices drifted from the hallway that led to the powder room and Bernard's suite, so Kaylee headed that way. When she got closer, she discerned the familiar rumble of the producer's voice along with the lighter tones of a woman.

"I'm not sure this is the time to talk about this," Bernard said. "We have a houseful of guests."

"But it can't wait." The woman's voice rose and Kaylee recognized Tanya. "I'm telling you I've figured something out. And it's important."

Kaylee's step hitched, but after a brief pause she kept going. What could possibly be more important than her message concerning Mervin's death? When she entered the hallway,

Bernard and Tanya were standing next to the bathroom door.

"Bernard," she said. "Sorry to interrupt, but the sheriff's department is here and a deputy wants to talk to you."

Tanya gasped, then recovered enough to say, "What is it now?"

Nick would want to see their unvarnished reactions to the news. "I'm not at liberty to say."

Bernard understood. "Let's go find out, shall we?"

Jocko had left, probably eager to get off the islet in the storm. Kaylee lingered while the deputy delivered the news to Bernard, his keen eyes never leaving the older man's face. Bernard took it in stride, but sorrow shadowed his eyes.

"I'm truly sorry to hear of this tragedy," Bernard said. "I knew Mervin for many years and obviously he was a close friend." His lips tightened. "First Gordon, and now this." He gave a tiny headshake. "Perhaps the balance of his mind was disturbed." One brow lifted, as did the inflection of his voice.

"We may never know exactly what happened," Nick said. "In this weather, the tides being what they are . . ." He didn't have to finish. Even if Mervin's body eventually washed up on shore, forensics might not be able to determine much, depending on the body's condition.

"I understand," Bernard said. He cleared his throat. "Should he be, er, located, please let me know. I'll do right by him. And poor Gordon. I'll plan memorial services and so forth for them."

"We appreciate that, Mr. Martin." His business concluded, Nick settled his hat on his head. "I urge you all to stay put tonight, or if anyone has to travel, do it now. We're issuing a travel advisory shortly. The storm is about to hit us full force."

Bernard opened the door for the deputy. "Take care of yourself out there, Deputy. Good night." He forced the door shut against the howling wind. "I'll send the guards home," he told Kaylee. "They won't be needed during this weather."

"I can't imagine any reporters braving this storm," Kaylee said. She was sure the men at the gate would appreciate being able to go home to their warm, dry houses. Now that Mervin wasn't a threat, she was sure the cruiser would also depart.

Travel and weather alerts began to pop up on people's phones, so the Petal Pushers and their spouses got ready to leave. "Are you sure you don't want to go home?" Mary asked Kaylee. "We can follow you."

"No, I'm going to stay," Kaylee said. "We're doing several more interior scenes tomorrow, and I need to freshen the flowers."

"All right, but keep in touch." Mary hugged Kaylee. To Bernard she said, "Thanks again for including us. We had a ball."

The others echoed her sentiment on the way out the door. In turn, the producer promised to invite them to the film's premiere. "I'm going to see if we can do it here on the island," he said. "We'll bring Hollywood to you. That will be fun."

"And lots of flower orders," Mary whispered to Kaylee with a wink.

Once the deputy and the extras were gone, everyone clustered around the fireplace in the great room, where Shane lit a roaring fire after moving the flower arrangements well away from the heat.

"Thank you, my good man," Bernard said to Shane. "Everyone, get refills of food and drink, and let's enjoy the fire's comfort. It's a bad night out there—and a sad one." As though to underscore his words, rain lashed at the tall windows.

Kaylee went to the dining room to get her first helping of food. With Nick's arrival, she hadn't had a chance to eat. Reese came up beside her while she was loading a plate with finger sandwiches and cut vegetables. He had taken off his suit jacket but still wore the dress shirt that brought out the blue of his eyes.

"How are you holding up?" he asked. Although Nick had spoken only to Bernard, the news about Mervin had traveled through the group within minutes.

His warm concern made tears sting her eyes. Hoping he hadn't noticed, she took a spoonful of potato salad and dumped it on her plate. "I'm okay. The news was shocking, though. I really hoped he'd turn himself in."

"Me too." Reese filled a plate with deviled eggs, tortilla chips and salsa, and vegetables. "But think about what this means. It's over, Kaylee. The ordeal is finally over."

As Kaylee poured a glass of ice water, she pondered his words. He was right. Mervin was gone, and that meant the case was closed. Then why wasn't she more relieved? Why did she sense that another shoe was about to drop?

Maybe because finding a boat adrift was hardly conclusive evidence that Mervin had gone into the water and wouldn't be coming back out.

Kaylee and Reese settled on a sofa on the fringe of the group. She picked up an egg salad sandwich and took a big bite, suddenly ravenous.

The others chatted about the shoot they'd just finished, led by Bernard, who resolutely kept the discussion away from Mervin.

Blair cuddled on a sofa beside Bernard. She still wore her stage makeup, the thick eyeliner forming raccoon rings. "It's going to take real acting on our part to pretend that we're on the outs," she told her fiancé. She lifted an almost skeletal wrist and patted his cheek. How much weight had she lost just since she'd arrived at Mukilteo?

Tanya grunted in derision, then hid a mocking smile in her glass. She'd been watching from the fringes, narrowed green eyes darting from face to face. "Lily didn't have to pretend," she murmured, loud enough for only Kaylee, seated nearby to hear.

Randall's eyes were also on the pair, but Kaylee couldn't read his expression. "I think we should record some of the storm," he said. "It will make great atmospherics." The wind screeched around the rooftop, lending credence to his idea.

Bernard glanced up at the cathedral ceiling, listening. "Good idea." He turned to Shane. "Why don't you set up a microphone to grab some of this?"

Shane, who'd been steadily eating while the others talked, nodded in agreement. "I can do that, boss. I'll video the trees flailing too."

Kaylee looked out the windows at the thrashing woods. She could imagine the scene in the film. It would be very effective. Then she realized something else. She needed to get to the cabin through that. Poor Bear must be wondering where she was.

"I'm headed for bed," Blair announced with a yawn and stretch. "I think I'm fighting off some kind of bug."

"Sleep well, my love," Bernard said. Despite his words, it was apparent that his mind was on something else.

Randall and Tanya soon exited too, and while Bernard, Reese, and Shane hooked up equipment, Amy began to clear away the food and dirty dishes. Kaylee decided to help, although she knew it was only delaying the inevitable. Once that was done, she'd force herself to venture out into the night.

"You think poor old Mervin offed himself?" Shane asked Bernard out of the blue. "Maybe he thought it was better than going to jail for the rest of his life."

Reese sucked in a breath but continued to work. Kaylee also cringed at the cameraman's insensitive comment, but she had to admit curiosity concerning Bernard's response. It was quite possible that someone had framed Mervin for Gordon's murder and then disposed of him.

Before the producer answered, Amy dropped the dish she'd been holding onto the table with a clatter. "What kind of remark was that? You're assuming he was guilty."

Shane shrugged. "But they found proof—"

"What? The hammer?" Amy waved a hand in dismissal. "Anyone could have used that." She strode toward Shane, her finger wagging. "Everyone was in that garage at one time or another. You, Randall, Tanya, even Blair." Amy's grief was transforming into something else—righteous anger. And she was correct. Perhaps the killer had worn gloves.

With a jolt of shock, Kaylee remembered the headband. Had the deputies ever gotten a good explanation from Blair concerning it?

Shane put up both hands, as though to ward Amy off. "But that reporter dude had photos."

"Photos can be faked," Amy said. "You of all people should know that. Who says Mervin was the last one on the beach?"

"Easy, Amy," Bernard warned. "We need to get through the next week, and it's hard enough already without dissension in the ranks."

Amy's response was to rip off her apron and throw it on the table. "All right then. I'll take my divisive self away." She stormed out of the room.

For a moment, there was only the sound of wind and rain battering the house. Then Bernard said, "She and Mervin were good friends, and Gordon's dead. I don't think any of us can blame her for being upset."

Kaylee could give him that point. But was Amy also right? Had Mervin been innocent? Pondering these questions, she continued to clean up. Amy didn't return. Kaylee loaded the dishwasher and put the food away. She didn't mind, really. Anything to delay going out into the storm.

"I'll walk you to the cabin." Reese strode into the kitchen. "It's not safe for you to go out there alone." He'd changed into jeans and his usual flannel shirt.

Kaylee wiped her hands on a dish towel. "But how will you get back here, then? It's not safe for you either."

Reese waved that off. "I'll be fine." He glanced over her outfit. "If you have something to change into, you might want to do that. I'll find you a rain slicker."

She glanced down at herself. He was right—she shouldn't let the nice garment get soaked and perhaps even muddy. Thankful she'd brought a change of clothing, she put on her jeans and slid her feet into the rubber-soled boots she'd worn earlier. The dress and shoes went into a plastic bag.

Reese brought her a bright-yellow rain slicker that was far too large, but at least it would protect her from the elements. Outside, the noises of the storm were almost deafening. Wind howled and branches creaked. Rain drummed on the roof and decks, creating rivers that snaked through the gardens and across the paths.

Kaylee clutched her bag and ducked her head against the onslaught. Only a short distance away from the house, the lights seemed like mirages. The surf was louder, and she pictured the beach under a fierce onslaught of waves.

They soon reached the cabin. Kaylee was thankful she'd left the porch light on so she could navigate up the steps. "Here I am. Thanks again, Reese." She was eager to get inside and take a long hot bath.

Reese walked her up the steps, watching while she dug out her key. He cocked his head. "Do you hear that?"

She listened, straining her ears. "I hear wind and waves." The sound of the water was even louder here, closer to the shore.

"Exactly. Something is wrong." Reese turned and began tramping down the steps.

Kaylee hesitated, torn between escaping inside and going with Reese. She unlocked the door, tossed the dress inside, and shut it again, with an apology to poor Bear, who was waiting right at the door for her to come in.

"Hold up, Reese. I'm coming," Kaylee called. She clattered down the steps, taking the last one at a leap. She landed on soggy leaves, slipped, and almost fell. She righted herself, shuddering. Normally she loved storms—their drama and excitement, the tinge of danger. Tonight she wasn't so sure.

He stopped and waited, his face a pale oval under his hood. "I'm not sure this is a good idea, Kaylee."

"If you can do it, I can." Kaylee moved faster, watching where she put her feet.

Reese didn't argue. Side by side, they slogged through the rain and wind. After a while, she figured out the trajectory of their route. They passed the house, then the gardens and greenhouses, and veered into the drive, where it was easier to walk, except for massive puddles.

The roar of the waves grew louder—at a point where it should have been diminishing. "Reese," Kaylee called. She didn't need to say more. In unspoken unison, they began to run.

They reached the gate. "Don't go any further," Reese shouted. "It might be dangerous."

Clutching the chain links of the gate, Kaylee strained her eyes into the darkness. Even with the driving rain and lowering clouds, she saw something truly terrible.

Less than a hundred feet away, a frothy mass of water churned and heaved—right where the causeway used to be.

16

Kaylee leaned against the gate, limp with horror and shock. This wasn't just a washed-out road. They were cut off from the rest of Orcas Island. Cut off from her home, her shop, everyone she knew, except Reese. Thank goodness Bear was with her. What if he'd been home alone?

"This is worse than I thought," Reese said. "The entire road is gone." His gaze was worried. "We're stranded, so I'll be in my guest room over the garage tonight. Good thing everyone else was over the causeway well before this happened."

"How long will it take for them to fix the road, do you think?" Kaylee asked. She couldn't tear her eyes away from the raging sea mere feet away.

"First the storm has to pass. Then hopefully the tide will go back to normal levels. Then they'll be able to get at the roadbed."

Kaylee's heart sank. "That might take days."

"Yeah. But once the weather clears, we can leave by boat, don't forget."

"What about our cars?" She supposed a barge might be able to ferry their vehicles. But what would that cost?

"Maybe they can put up a temporary bridge." Reese tugged on her arm. "Come on, let's get you back to Bear. We can't do anything about this tonight."

They plodded back up the drive, then skirted the house to reach the cabin. By the time they reached the tiny shelter, Kaylee was exhausted. "Take two," she said, trying to make light of it. Hearing her voice, Bear began to bark. "I'm coming, boy," she called.

"Get some rest, okay?" In the dull yellow glow of the porch

light, Reese looked like he needed to take his own advice. "Call me if you need to, no matter what time it is. I mean it."

Impulsively Kaylee gave Reese a hug. "I'll do that. I'm so glad you're here." She shuddered at the idea of being stranded without any of her friends. What would she have done then? She couldn't trust anyone else.

He gave her a salute. "Same here. What are friends for, right? Gotta share the tough times as well as the fun ones." With a laugh, he loped down the steps.

Kaylee went inside, shedding the soaking wet slicker by the door. Then she gave in to Bear's excitement, allowing him to leap into her arms, where he covered her face in doggy kisses, tail beating frantically. "I missed you too," she said, kissing the top of his head. "Let's go get a snack."

Bear enjoyed a bone while Kaylee plopped down in front of the fire, drinking a cup of hot tea and munching on a nut mix. The storm continued to rage on, the driving rain accented by the crash of thunder and lightning bolts that lit up the cabin. Alerts continued to go off on her phone: flood warnings, travel notices, and craft advisories. She silenced her phone. There was no use agonizing over something that couldn't be helped.

"It's going to be a long night," she told Bear. He finished his treat and hopped up beside her. Within thirty seconds, he was snoring. Maybe she should follow his example.

Driving rain and wind, not to mention thunder and lighting, woke her periodically throughout the night. But Kaylee found herself strangely rested the next morning anyway. The first thing she did was go to the window and gaze outside.

The storm damage was even worse in the light of day if that was possible. Tree branches, needles, and leaves littered the ground around the cabin. She was fortunate a tree hadn't fallen on the building. She glanced up at the ceiling. Nothing appeared to be leaking, which was more good news.

Then she shuffled into the bathroom and flicked the light switch. Nothing. She tried again, her heart sinking. The power was out. That was almost inevitable with this wind.

After washing up with cold water, she made coffee with boiling water and a small press, glad the stove was gas and still worked. Maybe they lost power on a regular basis out here. She got dressed, threw on the slicker, and made her way up to the main house, this time carrying Bear. She didn't want to leave him alone again during this frightening weather.

The lights were on in the house, and she heard the hum of a generator. Her steps quickened. Electricity meant heat. It also meant they could keep working on the film. That would be much better than being cooped up with nothing to do.

Kaylee went in through the back door, where she shed her raincoat and boots and set Bear on the floor. In her stocking feet, she padded through the deserted kitchen and into the dining area, Bear following. "Good morning, everyone," she said to the group seated around the table. Reese gave her a smile and wave of greeting while the others remained sunk in gloom, either staring at their phones or staring into space.

"Nothing good about it," Randall grumbled. "We're stuck here."

Bernard pressed his lips together. "Look at it as an opportunity to get some serious work done. Fortunately we have a generator and plenty of gas."

Shane nodded. "Yeah, good thing we've got juice. I've got some battery backups, but they don't last long."

Kaylee went to the sideboard and poured a cup of coffee. "The power went out at the cabin." She added cream and stirred, then checked out the platters of muffins and scones. Jessica must have brought them yesterday, before filming with the Petal Pushers.

"That's not surprising," Amy said. "There isn't a generator

there or in any of the outbuildings, except the greenhouses."

Considering the value of the orchids housed in the controlled environment, a generator was a good thing. Kaylee had seen whole nursery inventories destroyed by a power outage. That reminded her of the flowers in the laundry room cooler. Her first task after breakfast would be to maintain the arrangements in the great room.

Kaylee sat at the table next to Tanya. The actress sat slouched back in her chair, ankles crossed, while she sipped the bottled cold herbal tea she favored. "How are you this morning?" Kaylee asked, to break the gloomy silence that hung over the room.

In response, Tanya rubbed her midriff with a frown. "Not that great. Stomach's been upset all morning."

"Mine too," Blair piped up. As usual, she was drinking her green shake. "I've been so stressed out over Merv—" Clapping a hand over her mouth, she slid a glance at Amy. "Um, because of the storm, I mean."

Fortunately, Amy let the comment pass. After her outburst last night, everyone was probably walking on eggshells around her. Someone had gone to the trouble to set out breakfast, and Kaylee would bet it had been Amy, not one of the others.

Reese pushed back from the table with a sigh. "I'm going to head out and check the causeway, make sure the damage isn't spreading."

Shane hurriedly got up as well, no doubt eager to do something in a situation where they were basically all helpless. "I can't believe that happened," he said. "It blows my mind. Glad someone wasn't driving across right then."

"Me too," Randall said. "But we've seen worse in California. Whole hillsides coming down in an avalanche of mud and rocks."

"We're filming in an hour," Bernard called after them. "So make it quick. We're starting with one of your scenes, Blair and

Tanya. So run along and get ready, okay?"

Amy rose with a groan, putting one hand to her lower back. "I'll come do your makeup when you're ready."

The two women exchanged glances. "We'll do it ourselves," Blair said. "Take it easy, okay?"

Tanya linked her arm through Blair's. "It will give us a chance to catch up. I've hardly had time to talk to you, Blair. What with you getting engaged and everything."

The other actress gave a startled giggle. Until now Tanya had shown only disapproval regarding the match. "I'll show you the gown I've picked out. And I made a special page online for our wedding."

Remaining arm in arm, they strolled away, chatting like the best of friends. Kaylee wasn't the only one puzzled by this change in attitude on Tanya's part. Amy stared after them, then shook her head. Randall shifted uneasily in his chair. *Probably wondering if the two women are discussing him*, Kaylee thought with amusement.

After finishing a quick breakfast, Kaylee went to the laundry room to select flowers. She'd work on the urns where they sat, back in place flanking the fireplace. She was going through the buckets and pulling out the best blossoms when her phone rang.

"Hi, Mary," she said. "Guess what? We're stranded." It felt good to tell someone. "The causeway washed out last night, right after you guys left."

Mary's gasp of shock was gratifying. "That's horrible. Is everyone okay?"

"We're all fine. Reese thinks it will be a couple of days at least before they can do anything about it." Kaylee picked up her snips and trimmed leaves and the bottoms of the stems. "It's raining really hard and we're getting thunderstorms."

"Same here," Mary said. "I was thinking maybe we shouldn't open the shop. No one is supposed to be traveling. And wires are down in Turtle Cove's downtown."

That was an easy decision. "Stay home. I doubt we'll get any customers today anyway. Put a note on our social media that we're closed, okay?"

Before Mary could answer, Kaylee's phone went dead. She checked the battery. It still had juice, but there weren't any service bars. Annoyed, she set the phone on the counter. If wireless service was out, then the situation really was bad. That hardly ever happened.

A short while later, Kaylee carried an armful of flowers out to the great room. There she began to go through the arrangements, pulling out wilted blooms and replacing them with new ones. The front door opened with a burst of hearty male voices and a minute later the men trooped in. "Is the causeway still washed out?" she asked, knowing it was a ridiculous question.

"Yep, unfortunately," Reese said. "But the good news is that the damage isn't any worse. The tidal surge might even have gone down a little."

"Seeing something like that really makes you respect the power of water and wind," Randall said. "I guess I'd better go dry off." He strode from the room, whistling.

Reese came to crouch beside Kaylee, who was kneeling beside one of the urns. "Those arrangements sure are cheerful on a day like this."

Kaylee touched a dahlia blossom affectionately. "Working with flowers always makes me feel better, no matter what's going on." She slid the last stem of delphinium into the center, placing it to best effect. "By the way, my phone doesn't have any reception. You'd better check yours."

Reese dug in his pocket and pulled out a smartphone,

then fumbled with the screen. "Mine too. Great. The tower must be damaged."

Shane had been moving from window to window to check on the weather, which remained dismal. "I keep hoping this storm blows out to sea. It's supposed to at some point." He checked his own phone, then tapped it hard with his finger as though that would help. "What's up with this? I can't get service."

"There isn't any," Kaylee and Reese said in unison.

"Seriously?" Shane tapped the phone again, then gave up and slid it into his pocket.

Bernard strolled into the room. "Get the equipment fired up, Shane. We're going to start filming in a few."

The cameraman hurried to comply and, a few minutes later, Blair and Tanya appeared, made up and in costume.

"Are you two ready?" Bernard asked. He directed them to their positions, Blair on a sofa near the fire and Tanya by the doorway. She was to enter the room to wait on Blair. Then they would have a confrontation.

Kaylee and Reese moved out of camera range, Kaylee making sure Bear was staying quiet. He seemed content sleeping under the dining room table, where there was a strong possibility of crumbs coming his way.

Once filming had begun, Reese gestured for Kaylee to follow him into the laundry room, where they wouldn't disturb the actors. "Someone broke into Mervin's room," he said without preamble.

"What?" Kaylee blurted. She held up a hand when he started to repeat himself. "No, I heard you. It just surprised me. Tell me what happened." She'd been expecting another update on the storm.

Reese conveyed how he'd noticed Mervin's apartment door ajar when he went up to his room on his way back from checking out the causeway that morning. "At first I thought I was imagining things, that it was just a shadow. But no, it was open a crack. And someone had damaged the lock, so they didn't have the new key."

"Is anything missing?" Kaylee tried to picture the apartment. Why would someone go in there? Mervin didn't have many possessions, at least that she'd seen when she'd been in the room before.

"I couldn't tell. Nothing obvious was missing." Reese rubbed his chin, thinking. "I didn't tell the other two guys about it. Let sleeping dogs lie, right? I'll tell Bernard about it later."

"It wasn't that way when you got up this morning?" Kaylee asked, thinking it was more likely someone had broken in under the cover of night. Blair? She'd been in Gordon's room after his death. Could she have broken into Mervin's room too for some reason? But surely Reese or Shane would have heard that. Maybe. The storm was pretty loud.

"Not that I noticed. I might not even have looked in that direction." Reese rubbed his face, his features sagging in exhaustion. "I just don't remember."

"It's okay. It's good that you noticed it at all," Kaylee reassured him.

They returned to the set and, after the scene with Tanya and Blair wrapped, watched one with Bernard and Blair in the same setting. Then it was Tanya's turn again. Bernard sent Kaylee to get the actress, since she'd gone to her room to rest. "Tell her to be up here in half an hour."

Tanya was staying in the same wing as Blair. Kaylee noticed again how much quieter it was in the hallway, the sound muffled by carpets and thick walls. To her left were the bedroom doors.

Kaylee knocked on Tanya's door. No answer, so she knocked again, a little louder. She put her ear to the wood. Nothing. Maybe Tanya had already left the room.

Experimentally, she turned the knob, thinking she could see if that was the case.

The door swung open to her touch, revealing a dim room with drawn curtains. But a soft lamp burned on the bedside table, spreading light across the bed.

Where Tanya lay sprawled, terribly still.

17

Without conscious thought, Kaylee burst into the room and ran across the carpet. She reached for Tanya's wrist and checked for a pulse.

Nothing. The actress was dead.

Shock hit, making Kaylee's legs tremble. Her belly turned over and she swayed, light-headed.

Get it together. Kaylee bent over, resting her hands on her knees. She inhaled deeply a few times until she felt steadier. She straightened, forcing herself to observe the scene very carefully.

Several small objects rested in Tanya's other hand. Kaylee bent as close as she dared and saw they were some kind of seeds. Something tickled the back of her mind, a thought that escaped when she tried to grasp it.

She'd return to those later. She saw a handwritten note propped against the digital bedside clock. Conveniently placed, so no one would miss it.

Again without touching it, she bent to read.

I'm so sorry, all of you. But it's no use. The black hole wins. Too many losses. First my dear friend Lily and now Randall. I'll always love you, dear, but you belong with Blair, your soul mate.

Forgive me.

T.

Black hole? Had Tanya suffered from depression? If so, Kaylee was truly sorry. But something about this struck her wrong. Perhaps she didn't want to believe that a young, vibrant person on the cusp of a solid career would take her own life.

Now what? Kaylee considered. She needed to report this death to the authorities immediately. The cell phone was halfway out of her pocket when she remembered there was no service. Her gaze fell on the landline telephone on the other bedside table.

With a sigh of gratitude that Bernard had maintained the service, she picked up the receiver and dialed Nick's extension, praying that he was in the office. Yes, she could—and maybe should—go through the 911 switchboard, but no doubt they were inundated with storm-related problems.

Nick finally answered. "Hello, Kaylee." His voice was groggy, filled with a deep weariness. "We're going to get you out of there soon as we can. It's a nightmare right now."

"I appreciate that, Nick, but that's not why I'm calling." Kaylee went to the bedroom door and used her free hand to lock it. She didn't need any interruptions. "Tanya Ackerman is dead. Looks like suicide."

When he spoke again, she got the feeling that he was wide awake. "Say that again. Slowly."

"Turn on your recorder, okay?" She took him step-by-step through her discovery, then gave him a verbal tour of the room. It would be hours at best, a day more likely, before they could make it to the property. The seas were still too high for boats, and helicopters couldn't fly in the heavy winds.

"All right. This is what I want you to do." After confirming that the department wasn't able to get out there, he said, "I'm deputizing you according to *posse comitatus* law. You know what that means?"

"I do." Sheriff's departments had the right to deputize private citizens in case of emergency. She was already a consultant to the department so it wasn't much of a step, really.

"All right. Not that I want you making a citizen's arrest or anything. But you need to do some evidence collection and some crime scene documentation for us, just in case."

In case someone messes with the evidence. Kaylee sharpened her ears, knowing she'd need to remember every word. "Go ahead. I'm ready." She glanced at the clock. Bernard had said half an hour. Ten minutes had gone by. Only ten minutes? It felt like a lifetime.

"I want you to photograph the room, starting with the doorway, then moving in closer. You have my permission to examine one of those seeds, but I want you to put on gloves and bag and tag the rest, as well as the note. Do the same with anything else you think might be important."

From where she stood, Kaylee saw an empty bottle of tea on the floor. The brand Tanya liked. When she mentioned it, he said, "Bag that too."

Clicking sounded on the line. Fearing they were going to be cut off, she said, "Anything else? I should keep the room secured, correct? I'll have Reese change the lock."

"Yeah. Do that. And leave the body exactly where it is, okay? I know that's hard, but don't touch her."

Kaylee swallowed. "Okay. I think I've got it. By the way, I'm calling from the landline here. My cell phone isn't working."

Nick sighed. "I'm not surprised. One of the towers was hit and there isn't any service on one whole side of the island. Call me back later and let me know how you make out."

After she hung up, feeling as though she was relinquishing a lifeline, Kaylee did as he requested. Using her phone, she started from the doorway and took dozens of photographs. But no matter how closely she studied the scene, she found no evidence that anyone else had forced Tanya to take poison or hurt her in any other way.

Maybe something had been in the tea. But whether Tanya drank it purposely or by accident remained to be determined.

Twenty minutes were gone.

Kaylee used a pair of tweezers she found in the bathroom to pluck a seed out of Tanya's palm. She used an envelope from the writing desk to store it, then tucked it into her pocket.

The next challenge was bagging the evidence. She really didn't want to alert anyone else in the household until she was done, so if she didn't have to go to the kitchen all the better.

Her gaze fell on the bathroom sink. In the cabinet underneath, she found spare plastic bags and rubber gloves, which were presumably stored under there for whoever cleaned. She silently thanked whoever had stocked the place. Probably Amy.

Someone banged on the door. "Tanya? You in there?" It was Randall.

Her heart sank. She thought about ignoring him, but he began to jiggle the knob. "Hon, let me in."

Kaylee answered the door, only opening it a crack. "You can't come in, Randall. Tanya is . . . well, she's dead."

"What?" he roared. Lightning fast, his arm lashed out and pushed the door open, forcing Kaylee back. She stumbled and almost fell. Randall darted into the room. "Tanya! My love—"

"Don't touch her!" Kaylee shouted. "It's a crime scene."

He stopped inches away from the bed, pivoting around. "Did you kill her?" He took a few menacing steps toward her, his face twisted in a snarl. "If you did, I'll—"

Kaylee backed away from him. "No. Stop, please. I've been deputized. Call Deputy Nick Durham if you don't believe me."

"I will." Breathing heavily, he stormed around the bed and snatched the receiver. "What were you doing in here anyway?

That is seriously creepy."

"I'm collecting evidence." She gave him her best glare. "And you're contaminating the scene."

His response was to move his legs to a firmer stance as he dialed 911. While he did that, Kaylee put on the rubber gloves and bagged the note, bottle, and seeds, which she also lifted with tweezers, one by one.

Finally he slammed the phone down. "All right. I confirmed it, *Deputy* Kaylee." Fear and unease slid across his face. "Are you going to arrest me for disturbing the scene and threatening you?"

"Of course not. I know it's a terrible shock." Now that she had done what she'd promised Nick, the ebbing of adrenaline left her feeling shaky. "And I don't blame you for thinking the worst."

He edged away from his position by the bed, keeping his eyes resolutely away from Tanya. "Now what?"

"Now I have to inform the others. And secure this room." Kaylee thought for a moment. He needed something to do, and she needed to talk to someone she could trust. "Could you go get Reese for me?"

Kaylee waited for Reese outside the room, holding the bags of evidence. No doubt Randall would spread the news, but she couldn't do anything about that. What was critical was keeping people out until real law enforcement could arrive.

A few minutes later, she heard footsteps approaching rapidly. Reese appeared, followed closely by Bernard. "What's going on, Kaylee?" Reese asked. His features were set in grim lines.

As for Bernard, he moved delicately, as if he were barely holding himself together. "Not another one," he muttered. When Reese turned sharply in inquiry, he merely shook his head.

Kaylee opened the door and allowed the men to peek inside. "I found her like that. I phoned the sheriff—well, Deputy Durham. He instructed me what to do."

Reese's glance fell on the plastic bags she was clutching. "Evidence?"

"Yes. We need to keep it secure until they can get here."

"What do you want me to do?" Reese asked, folding his arms across his chest. "I'm guessing the sheriff doesn't want anyone in there."

"You got it, and they won't be able to get here until tomorrow at the earliest. Can you put a new lock on the door?"

Reese nodded. "I have some spare locksets with me."

"You really think someone might bother her?" Bernard shuddered.

"It's more that there may be trace evidence in there," Kaylee said. "The fewer people who go in there, the better."

"Hate to say it, but there's a real risk of someone messing around," Reese said. "Mervin's apartment was broken into. I've been meaning to tell you, Bernard."

"Broken into?" the older man exclaimed. "When?"

Reese put a hand on the wall and leaned. "Sometime this morning, I think. That's when I noticed it."

"My goodness." Bernard took a step back, using his cane to balance. "Who would do such a thing?"

"That's what I wonder." Reese nodded at the bags Kaylee was holding. "What's that note say?"

Kaylee held the bag so both could read the writing through the clear plastic. She didn't mention her suspicions that Tanya's death might not have been suicide. She knew from experience not to leap to conclusions. Besides, this was the fifth untimely death on this property. Or near this property, in the case of Mervin.

A thought dropped into her mind like a pebble into a pond. *What if Tanya figured out who killed Lily as she promised?* Kaylee shivered, making her hands shake. "Did you talk to Tanya?" she asked Bernard. "I heard her say she had something important to tell you."

The producer didn't answer. He was staring with wide eyes at the note, almost as if he were catatonic. "That note doesn't sound like Tanya. She was a pretty tough little nut."

Questions pressed against Kaylee's lips. Bernard was a major suspect. He had to be. Two of his young, healthy wives had died in accidents after both planned to leave him. And if Tanya had discovered a sordid truth, wouldn't someone want to make sure she never talked about it?

Reese reached up and rubbed the back of his neck. "I don't know her well, but maybe she was just good at hiding how she felt." He slid a glance at Kaylee, which told her he was trying to dampen speculation. It was safer for everyone to believe that Tanya had committed suicide.

Otherwise the killer might strike again.

Right now, in the middle of a huge storm on an inaccessible island, they were trapped like fish in a barrel.

"I'll go get my tools and change the lock," Reese said. "Then we'll make sure the keys are kept in a safe place."

"Maybe this project is doomed," Bernard said. "Maybe we should cut our losses. Circumstances outside our control."

Not sure if he wanted a comment, Kaylee kept quiet. The loss of three actors seemed pretty insurmountable to her, but what did she know? "So Tanya didn't talk to you?" she pressed.

Bernard shook his head. "No, I'm afraid not."

Kaylee studied the older man, wondering if he was lying. Maybe Tanya had discovered proof of Bernard's guilt.

The producer took a deep breath. "I guess we'll keep filming. While I've got Blair and Randall here, I might as well. I guess I'll go up. Give everyone the news and the update." He began shuffling away, his usual vibrant energy nowhere in evidence.

Reese waited until Bernard was out of earshot. "What's all that about?"

"I'm not sure." Kaylee sank to the carpet, cross-legged. While she waited for Reese to get his tools and the new lock, she could at least be comfortable.

"I'll only be a couple of minutes," Reese assured her. He started down the hall, then paused. "You know I don't believe in curses and all that hogwash. But whoever called this movie doomed is right."

With that cheery statement, he continued down the hallway. Kaylee leaned back against the wall. Now that she was alone and paying attention, she could hear the wind howling. How much longer would they be stranded here?

And how many of them would actually get to leave?

18

Reese returned quickly, as promised, Bear at his heels. He set down his toolbox and flipped the latches. "Someone was worried about you," he said with a grin, nodding to the dog.

Bear scrambled onto her lap and began to lick her face. She laughed and tried to dodge his tongue. "Cut it out, Bear. You act like I've been gone for days."

"Everyone knows about Tanya," Reese said. He used a utility knife to slash the plastic covering a lockset. "So you don't have to break the news or anything."

"Good. Although if I was a real deputy, I'd want to." Kaylee rubbed under Bear's chin, comforted by the dog's loving presence. "There is something I can do, though. I can try to identify the seeds Tanya was holding."

"Seeds?" Reese sent her a questioning glance. "I didn't see those."

"I put them in evidence but kept one to examine. Nick told me to try." Kaylee shifted, feeling the envelope in her pocket. "Tanya was probably poisoned. So those seeds might mean something." Again, a thought skittered. She tried to pin it down, but it slipped away.

"Where's your equipment?" Reese asked. "Out in the cabin?"

Kaylee considered her options. "All I have with me is my loupe." A microscope would have been better. "And I'll have to make do with guidebooks to plants I can find here in the library. I won't be able to get online." It was a challenge, for sure.

"I'll walk you out there whenever you want. You're not going anywhere alone again, not while we're here."

Warmth flooded Kaylee at his protective words. She was so fortunate to have him here with her. At least someone cared about her safety and well-being.

After putting on gloves, Reese unscrewed the old knob and pulled it out, exposing a round hole in the door. "I thought we should put on a new knob so the sheriff's department can try to get prints from this one," he explained. "I hope I didn't smudge all of them, if there are any."

"Good thinking," she said as she helped him bag it. "So how did everyone seem?" She still didn't want to go out to the main room and face the others. She'd seen Randall and Bernard's reactions. Neither had been pleasant, although Bernard's response had been odd, almost cold. He hadn't been overtly angry and grieving like Randall. She told Reese about her encounter with the actor.

"Randall's still pretty upset," Reese said. "I don't blame him, though."

"How's Blair?" Kaylee asked.

Reese lifted his head. "I want to get her away from Bernard and talk to her. We've got a lot to discuss." He slid the new doorknob in. "And I want you to be there."

After Reese was finished, Kaylee insisted he keep a key, as the only person on the property she trusted. As temporary deputy, she kept the other on her person. They stowed the bags of evidence inside the room, near the doorway, and locked it. Then Kaylee mounted a handwritten sign on the door: *Sealed by order of the Sheriff's Department.*

Reese escorted Kaylee and Bear out to the cabin. "I wish we didn't have to do this," she shouted above the driving rain. "It's awful." She vowed to keep her loupe in her tote from now on. But who could have guessed she would need it?

"Me too," Reese shouted back. "Let's hurry."

At the cabin, the power was still out and the air was chilly. "I'll light a fire," Reese said. He glanced at the gas stove. "And how about a cup of coffee? Sound good?"

"Absolutely," Kaylee said, shedding her slicker. She rubbed Bear down with a towel so he wouldn't catch a cold. He trotted off to sit beside the stove, which soon emitted toasty heat.

Kaylee found her loupe in her luggage, and placed it and a couple of guidebooks on the table. She dug the envelope out of her jeans pocket and dumped the seed onto another sheet of paper.

The small oval was fleshy, which gave her a clue. She studied it with the loupe. Yes, it was actually what was called an aril, a coating which helped the seed float. Eventually the aril would disintegrate, allowing the seed to sink and root in the bottom of a body of water.

"This is a water lily seed," she said to Reese.

He poured boiling water into the press. "Are those poisonous?"

"Not at all." But Kaylee could guess their significance. "I think Tanya, or perhaps someone else, is pointing to Lily—and her death." The pool where she had drowned was now filled with the pretty but invasive plants. "She told me she was trying to find out why Bernard's wives have a habit of dying."

Reese grabbed two mugs from the cupboard. "She believed Lily's death wasn't an accident?"

"That's what she told me. I think she was also wondering about Audrey falling off that cliff." Kaylee looked at Reese, noticing his face was ashen. "We need to warn Blair."

He nodded. "I didn't like the whole setup already or what it's doing to her. But if she's in actual danger—" He clunked two cups of coffee on the table. "After you're done, let's go find her."

While they drank coffee, Kaylee took pictures of the seed and wrote up a brief report concerning her conclusions. An autopsy would be needed to determine how Tanya died. *Something in the tea, perhaps.* Tanya had been complaining of feeling ill at breakfast. The lab might be able to find traces of poison or medications in the bottle Kaylee had salvaged.

She pushed aside her half-finished coffee. "Let's go. I also need to check in with Nick. I have to do that at the house, on the landline." She gazed at Bear, content by the fire, and found herself envying his peace. "Let's leave him here."

They emerged into the wind and rain, which if anything was even worse. Kaylee pictured the movement of the storm, the way it circled around, bringing periods of heavy activity again and again.

To Kaylee's right, light flickered in the trees. "There it is again." She tugged on Reese's arm. "See. Someone is in that cabin. The Lily Pad."

Reese frowned. "Let's go check it out." He took the path leading in that direction.

Kaylee followed, wincing as wind tossed the trees overhead. She prayed a branch wouldn't fall and hit them. Twigs and small branches were everywhere, making it hard to walk.

They paused in the clearing in front of The Lily Pad. A light flickered in the window—a candle, Kaylee realized. The electricity was out here too. A thread of smoke drifted from the chimney, carrying an odor of wood smoke.

"Let's go see who it is." Reese squared his shoulders and marched toward the cabin.

"Be careful," Kaylee said. "Maybe it's—" She couldn't finish the thought, it was too ridiculous. Mervin was gone, washed out to sea.

Reese crept up the steps, moving softly so the person inside wouldn't hear. Heart in her throat, Kaylee followed. Reese edged along the wall to a window and peered inside. He gestured for Kaylee to join him.

Jocko McGee sat on a futon, scribbling furiously on a lined pad of paper. His socks and shoes were placed in front of the stove, probably to dry.

"What is he doing here?" Kaylee asked. The last time she'd seen him was when he'd been taking stills and publicity shots. She'd assumed he'd left at the same time as the Petal Pushers.

Reese didn't bother to knock. He opened the door and walked in, followed by Kaylee.

Jocko jumped, sending his pad and pen flying. "Hey, what are you doing?" the reporter demanded.

"I guess I could ask you the same," Reese said. "You're trespassing."

Although the cabin was lit only by candles, Kaylee plainly saw Jocko's thoughts pass across his face. He was trying to figure out the most palatable explanation. "I was stranded," he finally said.

Kaylee scoffed. "Sorry, I'm not buying it. I've seen the lights on in here more than once, starting before the storm. You've been camping out."

"Without permission, I'm guessing," Reese added.

Exhaling a huge breath, Jocko slumped back against the cushion. He didn't meet their eyes. "Busted. Yeah, I'm here working on a story. Saw this place was empty, so I decided to hang out." He retrieved his pen and tapped it on the coffee table. "I'm not hurting anyone."

Reese turned toward the door. "I'm afraid I'm going to have to report you. Let's go, Kaylee."

"Wait." Jocko sprang to his feet, sending the pen flying again. "Don't do that. I'm on the trail of a killer. I've almost got it all put together."

Kaylee laid a hand on Reese's arm to stop him. "Let's hear him out."

"All right," Reese said. "We'll give you five minutes."

"Thanks, man." Jocko shuffled over to the table in the kitchen nook. "Come over here and I'll explain."

Kaylee and Reese shed their dripping slickers and joined the reporter. Jocko put aside some folders, revealing a poster board with photographs and notes covering it. He held it up so they could see it better.

After a minute, Kaylee figured out what she was looking at. Jocko was investigating the deaths of Audrey and Lily, with theories and lines connecting the people involved. "You think those women were murdered."

"I do." Jocko ran a hand through his unruly hair. "To be honest, I got the idea from Tanya Ackerman. One night she kind of forgot I was a reporter and spilled the beans. She was convinced someone killed Lily."

"Was that here?" Kaylee asked.

"Nope. A few months ago, in LA. Right after she got the part in this picture."

And now Tanya was dead. Kaylee glanced at Reese, who shook his head ever so slightly. Instead of telling Jocko about Tanya's death, she asked, "So who do you think is guilty?"

Jocko's eyes narrowed. "Not to go past this room, okay?" At their nods, he said, "Bernard Martin." He jabbed a finger at the poster, to the lines running between Bernard and his wives. "In both cases, they were getting ready to divorce him, which would have been financially catastrophic due to community property laws. So he killed them."

Kaylee couldn't argue. She'd suspected the same thing.

A few minutes later, Kaylee and Reese continued their interrupted trek to the house. They'd decided to leave Jocko alone for now. Once access to the property was restored, Reese had informed him that he was to leave immediately.

"Do you believe his theory?" Kaylee asked. It made a terrible kind of sense. Bernard was the common denominator in all these deaths.

"I don't know if I do or not," Reese said. "But everything that happens only makes me more afraid for Blair."

Perhaps the two wives *had* died in accidents and Jocko—and Tanya—were wrong. But if they were right, then marrying Bernard would put Blair squarely in a killer's sights. Unless Bernard was guilty, and Blair stayed with him forever. Then he'd have no reason to kill her. Kaylee sighed in frustration. Would they ever learn the truth?

Reese glanced over at her. "We're almost there," he said.

"It's not that. I'm just so confused about this whole situation." They reached the back door and slipped inside with relief, shedding slickers and boots there.

"Where is everyone?" Reese asked. The place was silent, with a deserted feeling hanging over the house. Even Amy wasn't in the kitchen as usual.

"They must be holed up in their rooms," Kaylee said. No doubt they were locked in, waiting for the storm to pass so they could escape. That's what she'd be doing if she didn't have the task of investigating Tanya's death.

She picked up the kitchen phone, glad to hear the dial tone. "Let me give Nick an update." Reese nodded, and Kaylee punched in the number.

Nick answered immediately. "How are you holding up? I'm sorry we can't get you out of there yet. The helicopter is still grounded, and forget about using a boat."

"I understand. I have some information for you." As Kaylee filled him in, she studied Reese, who was pacing around the kitchen. He was anxious to talk to his cousin, and she didn't blame him.

"You're doing great," Nick said at the end of the report. "Call me if you get anything else, okay? Be careful."

"Will do," Kaylee said, then ended the call.

By mutual unspoken consent, Kaylee and Reese went to the bedroom wing to find Blair. Reese knocked on her door. "Blair. I need to talk to you."

Silence. For a sickening moment, Kaylee pictured Blair lying dead on the bed. Reese knocked again. "If you don't answer, I'm going to take the door off the hinges."

Kaylee heard a thump and the sound of shuffling footsteps, accompanied by muttering. The knob rattled as Blair unlocked it. "What?" the actress asked, squinting against the hall light. She'd pushed a sleep mask up on top of her head, and her blonde hair stuck out every which way. "No need to go all caveman on me. I was napping."

"I can see that," Reese said. He pushed past her into the room. "We need to talk to you."

"It's important, Blair," Kaylee said gently, trying to soften Reese's blunt insistence.

Blair shut the door behind them and locked it. Then she folded her arms across her chest and frowned. "Go ahead, say what you need to. You've been dying to lecture me for days."

"It's not about that," Reese said. "You're a grown woman and can make your own decisions. But I love you, and I have to tell you I have real concerns—"

They would get nowhere if Blair felt she was being treated like a child. "Blair," Kaylee interrupted. "We really need to talk to you. Not just about your engagement."

"Which you need to break," Reese said. "Unless you want to become the third late Mrs. Martin."

Blair's mouth dropped open. "That's what Tanya said to me. And now she's—" She staggered to the bed and collapsed on it. "What is going on around here?"

"That's what we'd like to know." Kaylee sat in an armchair.

"Tanya believed Lily was murdered. And she wasn't the only one who felt that way." She decided not to mention Jocko by name.

"But they said she drowned." Blair's shoulders hunched and she shivered. "Is there any proof of something different?"

Reese glanced at Kaylee. "Nothing definitive at this time. But you have to wonder if maybe Tanya stumbled on to something."

Blair rubbed her arms. "But I thought she killed herself. That's what Randall said. He said she left a note."

So he had noticed that. During the tense scene in the room, Kaylee hadn't been sure. "She did leave a note." Kaylee hesitated. Should she tell Blair what it said? Then she decided to go ahead. There were too many secrets, hints, and innuendos.

"She said she was releasing Randall so you two could be together." Having made the statement, Kaylee stood back mentally to see the results.

Blair laughed. "What? You're kidding." She ran both hands through her hair. "Me and Randall? That's been over for ages."

Something in her voice didn't ring quite true. Kaylee plunged ahead with other questions. "What were you looking for in Gordon's room?"

"Gordon's room? You didn't tell me about that," Reese said.

"I know. And I didn't mention that the sheriff found Blair's headband next to Gordon's body."

Reese glared at his cousin. "Fess up, Blair. Now. I can't help you if I don't know the whole truth."

Blair cringed back on the bed. "I'm sorry. I didn't think it mattered." She put up both hands as though warding off Reese's anger. "I didn't kill Gordon. Yes, I talked to him that morning. My headband must have fallen off. I wondered where it went."

"Gordon knew something that didn't reflect well on you, didn't he?" Kaylee guessed. "Was it something to do with Randall?"

"No." Blair's voice was tiny. "Bernard. You see, I asked

Gordon to introduce us. After Randall and I broke up, I had to think about my next move." She attempted a smile. "Bernard happened to be in town, working on a new project. I wanted to be part of it."

Kaylee remembered the official story, that their introduction had been random chance, serendipitous and fated. But Blair had engineered it in a calculating and perhaps cold way. If Bernard learned that, he might think the same about the engagement. *And he wouldn't be far off the mark.*

Reese sank down into a chair. "You took it a little further than just a part in a movie."

"I did, didn't I?" Blair's face shone with pride. "He fell in love with me right off, and I would have been stupid to discourage him. He's going to make me a star."

"Like he did Lily and Audrey?" Kaylee asked quietly.

The actress winced as though Kaylee had tossed cold water over her. "Yes, like that."

"It didn't work out that well for them in the long run," Reese said gently.

Blair's face paled. "True. But I'm not going to die." Her voice shook, belying her own words.

"You might if we don't figure out who killed Lily and Audrey," Reese said. He opened his mouth to say more, then clamped it shut.

Kaylee guessed he had almost shared the suspicion that Bernard was behind the deaths. But if he was, it wouldn't be wise to mention it to anyone. Not while they were trapped here.

When they left Blair's room a few minutes later, they heard the snap of the lock behind them. "I hope some of what we said sank in," Reese said. "But I'm not counting on it." His shoulders slumped in discouragement.

Kaylee felt equally gloomy. "Let's go get something to eat."

Maybe some food would help lift her depression and anxiety. She was counting the minutes until they could leave this place.

In the kitchen they foraged for sandwich fixings, which they ate in the dining area. The great room was still deserted, with only the ceaseless wind keeping them company.

"I'm about ready to leap out of my skin," Kaylee said. She crunched a chip.

"Me too." Reese pulled out his phone, then smacked himself on the forehead. "I wanted to check the weather, but we still have no Internet."

Kaylee glanced out the window. "The forecast is for rain. And wind." She laughed, surprising herself. Reese joined in. "You just have to laugh sometimes."

"You bet." Looking marginally more cheerful, Reese pushed back from the table. "Shall we go check on Bear?" He picked up their empty plates.

While she was pushing her feet into her boots, Kaylee remembered the recipe box that recorded dietary preferences. There might be something useful in there regarding the specific diet Tanya ate. "Hold on, Reese. I'm going to get something."

She retrieved the recipe box and put it in her slicker pocket. Then something else niggled at her mind. "Can we take the evidence out of Tanya's room? I'll feel better if it's at Hideaway."

Reese agreed. They retrieved the evidence envelopes, tucked them into a waterproof zippered tote, and resealed the room, then headed outside. Afternoon was wearing on, and soon it would be dark. They trudged along the path, avoiding puddles and fallen branches.

Something lay on the ground up ahead. Kaylee narrowed her eyes, trying to discern what it was. *A person.* Someone was lying on the ground.

Reese gave a shout and broke into a run. Kaylee sloshed along behind him, not able to move quickly in her boots. By the time she caught up with Reese, he was hunkered down beside Shane.

The cameraman wasn't moving.

19

"Is he all right?" Kaylee asked.

The cameraman lay facedown. He was wearing a raincoat, but his legs and feet were soaking wet. How long had he been out here?

"He's got a good strong pulse," Reese said. He shook the young man's shoulder gently. "Shane. Can you hear me?"

To Kaylee's relief, Shane groaned and rolled onto his side. He tried to sit up then collapsed back, his face etched with pain. "Ouch. My head."

Reese picked up a good size branch lying nearby. "This must have hit him."

Shane closed his eyes. "Yeah, that's it. I think. Something hit me."

"Get Jocko," Reese said. "We've got to get Shane inside."

Kaylee hurried to The Lily Pad, flinching whenever the wind gusted. All she needed was to have a branch fall and hit her too.

Thankfully Jocko answered her knock immediately. "What's up?" he asked, scratching his head.

"Shane, the cameraman, is injured, and we need your help. We're taking him to my cabin." As she said it, she realized that was the best option, since her cabin was closer than the house.

"Let me put on some shoes." Leaving the door open, Jocko crammed his feet into a pair of sneakers, then grabbed a jacket. Neither was adequate against the weather, but Kaylee didn't bother to say anything.

"He fall down or something?" he asked as they trotted along the trail.

"We think a branch hit him on the head. He's conscious now,

thankfully." Kaylee had no idea how they would have moved an unconscious man.

With Jocko and Reese holding him up, Shane was able to totter to the cabin. "It was the strangest thing," he said once inside, wrapped in a blanket in front of the stove. "I thought I saw something out of the corner of my eye, then *wham*!"

A falling branch—or a cane? Bernard, an actor as well as a director, wasn't nearly as unsteady on his feet as he sometimes appeared. But why hit Shane? Kaylee used a towel to gently dry his hair. Thankfully, the scalp hadn't been broken. She tossed the towel in the hamper, then retrieved the recipe card box from her pocket and set it on the table.

Reese checked Shane for symptoms of concussion. "You're going to have a big bump and a headache, but that's all," he concluded. "You sure are lucky."

Shane tried to crack a grin. "My mom always said I had a hard head."

Kaylee gave him some over-the-counter painkillers from her purse and a glass of water. "Take it easy for a while and enjoy your new friend." Bear had climbed on the sofa and was curled up close to Shane.

"You're a good boy, aren't you?" Shane stroked Bear's chin, then settled back with a groan. "I could go for a nap right about now."

"One more thing." Reese loaded more wood into the stove and stirred the coals. "Why were you out in this weather?"

His eyes already closed, Shane mumbled, "Going up to the Aerie. Bernard wants to do some filming up there. Guess he'll have to run the camera now. He made me take the equipment up earlier."

"The Aerie. Is that the place up on the hill?" Kaylee asked.

Jocko, who'd been busy making coffee in the press, answered. "It is. You haven't been up there? Fabulous view."

"Not yet," Kaylee said. She moved closer to the fire, allowing the warmth to seep into her bones. Bernard's determination to keep going on the film was verging on the ridiculous. But maybe it was something to hold on to in the face of his losses.

"You know what's weird?" Jocko said. "Tanya was supposed to come down to The Lily Pad this afternoon. But she never showed. You guys see her at the house?"

Silence fell, broken only by Shane's snores, as Kaylee struggled with what to tell him. Reese's face displayed the same indecision. Finally Reese said, "This is off the record, okay? Her family doesn't even know yet. Tanya is dead."

Jocko deflated visibly, the air seeming to leave his body. "Tanya?" His voice cracked. "No. What happened?"

Kaylee gave him a brief summary. "I've been deputized, but this is not an official statement," she reminded him.

He held out his hands. "So you'll arrest me if I blab?" He gave a weak laugh. "Sorry. It's just that I'm in shock."

"We all are," Kaylee said.

Reese touched her arm. "I'm stepping out for more wood." A small shed next to the house held stacks of firewood. Reese picked up the wood sling and headed outside.

A minute later he burst through the door again, the sling dangling empty and a panicked expression on his face. "The house is on fire! I saw smoke rising above the trees."

Leaving Shane asleep, Kaylee, Reese, and Jocko pounded along the trail up to the house. For once, Kaylee successfully ignored the cold rain lashing her face. She was too busy praying for those who might be inside, for the property not to be destroyed, and especially for poor Tanya's body. They'd quickly hidden the evidence in her cabin, in a storage closet under the loft stairs, before they left.

They slowed when they reached the back lawn. Tendrils of

smoke were still drifting in the air, but they had dwindled.

"That's strange," Reese said. "Maybe it was the chimney."

Jocko stared up at the roof. "I don't think so. Nothing's coming out of it now."

Reese trotted toward the deck. "Let's go inside and figure this out." He slipped in through the French doors, Kaylee and Jocko behind him.

Again, Kaylee had the sense that the house was empty. All the lights were still off and the kitchen was more or less as they had left it, though she did see the blender jar Amy used for smoothies in the sink. "Where is everyone?"

"You think at the Aerie?" Reese asked. "Maybe they all went up there already. Kaylee, will you go see if Blair is still here? We'll take the lower level."

Kaylee went down the bedroom wing, knocking on each door. No one answered. Blair's door was open slightly, but the actress was gone. Tanya's door was still secure.

She went to find the others and found them standing in the lower hallway outside Bernard's office. By the pungent odors she inhaled as she approached, Kaylee guessed this was where the fire had originated. The odor of charred papers and books on the desk confirmed it. "What made it go out?" she asked.

"Sprinkler system." Reese pointed upward. The water had stopped, but everything in the office was damp. "Good thing it has zones or the whole house would be soaked."

"Who could have set the fire and why?" Kaylee asked. She couldn't imagine who among the remaining residents would want to burn Bernard's office and perhaps the whole house as a result.

"I have no idea, but I think we'd better go find everyone," Reese said. He continued to study the sprinkler system. "You know another good thing? I bet that system was hooked up to the landline and called the fire department. We could use a little backup about now."

If they can get to the property. "I need to call Nick again," Kaylee told the others. "It will only take a minute." She went upstairs to use the kitchen phone. This time Kaylee got voice mail. She left a message summarizing the latest events, including Shane's injury, the attempted fire, and their plan to go to the Aerie.

"Do you know the way?" Kaylee asked Reese once they left the house.

"There are two choices," he said. "We can go the longer way around on the back drive, or we can take the woods path."

The road would offer better footing, but Kaylee was eager to get to the Aerie. "Let's take the trail."

Partway there, Kaylee heard a strange sound—from her pocket.

"Is that your phone?" Reese asked.

"I think so." Kaylee stopped under the shelter of a huge Douglas fir and fumbled for the phone. The two men stopped to wait while she answered. "It's Nick," she said. "Hey, you called me on my cell! That must mean the service is working."

"Yeah, off and on," he said. "I tried the house but no one answered."

"That's because no one is there." She quickly filled him in and explained where they were headed. "We want to make sure everyone is okay."

"Be careful," Nick said. "There's a reason I called." He paused. "We believe Mervin survived the capsizing of his boat. A witness came forward and said he saw a man swimming toward shore. When he got to land, he took off."

"Mervin is alive?" Kaylee blurted, causing both Reese and Jocko to stare at her. "Is that a warning?"

"Of course it is." Nick sounded somber. "I don't know what game he's playing, but it doesn't take much insight to realize he's probably headed your way." Another pause. "If he's not there already."

"I'll stay in touch. Please try to get here soon. We're at our wit's end."

"We're doing everything we can."

After she hung up, she said, "Did you two get that? Mervin is alive and probably in the vicinity."

Jocko took a step backward. "Whoa. Do you think he set the fire?"

"That fits." Reese stared up the trail, where the lights of the Aerie winked. "All the more reason to get up there fast."

They began walking up the trail again, ducking their heads against the wind. A section of the path emerged from the trees, running along a slippery ledge. The gusts were so strong here that Kaylee had to hold on to Reese's slicker, since the wind had enough force to make her lose her footing. The wet rocks didn't help with that. Behind them, Jocko walked with arms out, legs braced, moving step by careful step.

Halfway across, she realized. *This is where Audrey fell.* Her eyes went toward the edge, only a couple of feet away. On a sunny day, the view must be spectacular from here. But now the neighboring islands were lost in the twilight.

Another blast hit her full force, making her stagger. "Hang on," Reese yelled. "We're almost there." He grabbed her arm and pulled her to the shelter of the trees. "If I'd realized how close the trail went to the cliff, I would have taken the road."

"Me too." Kaylee stared back at the outcropping, thinking of Audrey. It would take so little for someone to have pushed her off-balance. One well-placed tap of a cane? She shoved aside the thought. There were living people who might need help right now.

Jocko lingered on the rocks, staring out at the view. When

Reese called to him, his distant expression told Kaylee he'd been thinking about Audrey too.

Now the trail switchbacked up the hillside, revealing glimpses of the Aerie from certain points. Kaylee moved steadily along, both reluctant and eager to reach the cabin. What would they find there? The dread seeping into her bones was surely a warning.

They halted in a clearing below the cabin. A large deck protruded from the A-frame building, which was fronted with huge windows. Kaylee saw movement in the brightly lit space, but that was all. If someone glanced outside, what would they see? Three huddled figures in rain slickers?

"I don't think I want to go marching right up to the door," Jocko said.

"Yeah," Reese agreed. "Let's get the lay of the land first." He studied the property, then pointed up the hill, where a couple of vehicles sat in a level area. "That way."

This last little hill was steep but open, a cleared area made when the cabin was built. Kaylee's heart was pounding by the time they reached the parking area, from exertion and nerves. They stood under an overhang to catch their breath.

"Now what?" Jocko whispered. Beside them was a door that led into a kitchen area. He reached a hand out, as though planning to enter.

Reese grabbed the other man's wrist. "Don't. I'm going to try to get a look at what's going on."

A short set of steps led onto the deck and Reese led them up those. Windows provided glimpses of the interior to their left, first the kitchen and then a dining area. Maybe Bernard lived up here sometimes when he was working on an especially consuming project. When they reached the third window, Reese stopped short. Kaylee ran into him.

"Sorry," he whispered. He pointed into the room.

Bernard lay facedown on the wood floor. Beyond him stood Amy. Blair and Randall occupied two straight chairs facing her.

"What are they doing?" Kaylee whispered. Why weren't they helping Bernard?

Jocko also pressed close to the window and gasped. "She's got a gun."

Amy moved slightly and Kaylee saw Jocko was right. She was holding a pistol pointed steadily at the couple. Reese put a finger to his lips and sidled to the next window. There he studied the situation before creeping back to join them.

"She's making them drink green smoothies." His expression was puzzled. "What's that all about?"

Kaylee realized what was going on all at once. "She's poisoning them." She thought about Blair's habit of drinking the thick, green concoction. Many actresses did that to stay slim and healthy. Tanya had her tea—another habit. Amy had a garden. Many plants could help, but they could also harm.

Jocko stared bug-eyed at the murderous assistant. "Amy did it. She did it all. I bet she's even the one who killed Lily and Audrey." He lowered his voice to a harsh whisper. "Think about it. If you're drugged, it's real easy to drown or fall off a cliff."

Kaylee leaned against the building. With his words, the truth fell into place like puzzle pieces finally fitting together. "Do you think she killed Gordon too?"

"Naw. That was me." Mervin appeared from among a thick group of evergreens. He also held a gun, and this one was pointing right at them. "I think we'd better join the party, don't you?"

20

Reese and Mervin stared at each other for a long, fraught moment. "How do I know that's real?" Reese asked. "Maybe it's a prop."

"Oh it's real," Mervin said with a smirk. "Just because I used fake ones in my movies doesn't mean I don't know how to shoot." He waved it again. "Go on. Open that back door."

"Kaylee, I'm so sorry," Reese muttered, his hand slowly moving to the doorknob. She sensed his mind ticking over, trying to find a way out of this.

"Shut up," Mervin said. He trotted closer to them. "Go on. I'm getting a little impatient here."

"Why are you doing this, man?" Jocko asked. "We never did anything to you."

Mervin barked out a laugh. "You have a short memory for a hack. I remember quite a bit of coverage about my downfall in your rag."

"Great," Reese said. "What'd you do that for, Jocko?" His tone was ironic.

"That wasn't even me," Jocko protested. "Besides, we all just write what the editor wants."

"Did you hit Shane?" Kaylee asked Mervin. The cameraman had claimed to see something right before getting hit. Maybe it had been the escapee.

A sly expression slid over Mervin's face. "What if I did?" Then the smirk slid from his face again. "Open that door. Now."

Reese twisted the knob and pushed the door open, and Mervin herded them inside. At the sound of footsteps, Amy looked away from her victims. Blair and Randall followed her gaze, their eyes widening with hope. At this distance, Kaylee could see that they were tied to the chairs, but each had one arm free, holding a covered cup of green sludge.

"I wouldn't come in here, if I were you." Amy's veneer of meek, helpful assistant was gone, leaving the malice and anger Kaylee had glimpsed a few times and misinterpreted as grief. "Unless you want to join these two."

"I brought 'em," Mervin said, stepping around the taller Jocko. "I got a bone to pick with you, lady."

At the sight of the armed man, the captives' faces tightened in confusion and fear.

Amy gasped, her fingers slipping on the gun. Unfortunately, she regained control of it. "I thought you were dead. The sheriff said they found your boat—"

Mervin cut her off. "Did you think that was a good thing?" He trod closer, moving with soft footsteps like a prowling panther. "Everyone thought I was dead. I wanted them to." He grinned. "You fools didn't even know I slept in my own bed."

Kaylee realized it was Mervin who had broken into his own apartment.

"Of course it wasn't a good thing when you disappeared." Amy dragged a hand through her hair, which was already in disarray. "I was devastated when we heard they found your boat drifting."

"Why? Because I didn't live to serve my sentence?" Mervin's voice was a low, dangerous growl. Like his coworker, he had shed all semblance of civility. "This is all your fault, Amy. You know that."

Reese tensed as if for a leap.

The chauffeur whirled, cocking the gun. "Don't try anything. I'm warning you."

Reese put his hands up. "All right. Take it easy."

Kaylee bent to check Bernard. To her relief, his pulse was strong. Judging by the blood on the back of his head, he'd been struck and knocked out.

While crouched down, she took advantage of her position to turn on her cell phone recorder. She thought about dialing Nick and letting him listen, but she couldn't risk anyone hearing his voice when he answered. Would she get a good recording from her pocket, though?

Inspiration struck. She pulled the phone from her pocket and slid it behind a table leg, where their captors hopefully wouldn't see it.

Amy dropped her stare from Mervin and focused on Kaylee where she knelt beside Bernard. "Leave him," she barked. "I'll take care of Mr. Martin." Her mouth twisted in a feral grin. "He's finally all mine."

Mervin stood in front of Blair and Randall, a smirk dancing across his features. "What's all this about? Having a little snack?"

"She's trying to make us drink this stuff," Blair said, her voice shaking. "I think it's poisoned."

"Murder-suicide is my guess," Randall said. "Wrap it all up with a neat little bow."

Mervin spun to face Amy. "Why didn't I see it before? *You* killed Lily and Audrey. They both loved your little green drinks. You were jealous of them." His lip curled in derision. "Like you're jealous of Blair."

Blair gave a high-pitched wail. "Oh, Randall. I'm so sorry."

"Sorry for what?" Randall asked with a wry smile. "Leaving me or getting involved with Bernard?"

"Both." Her wail turned into sobs. "I've made so many mistakes."

With a snarl, Amy jostled Mervin aside and pushed her

face close to Blair's. "You can say that again. Always thinking about yourself and your precious career. Just like those other two floozies." She cocked her head, regarding Bernard with fondness. "He's so dumb. He never could see that you and the others were just using him."

"Did you kill Tanya too?" Kaylee asked loudly. She figured she might as well get the truth while she had the chance. Somehow they would get out of this jam, and this heartless killer would be brought to justice.

She couldn't entertain any other possibilities.

Amy smirked. "Obviously. That little hussy was on to me. I don't know how she managed to put two and two together. Not bad for a birdbrain."

"You drugged her tea, didn't you?" Kaylee accused. "That's your modus operandi, making people vulnerable with some kind of herbal concoction." *Then drowning Lily and pushing Audrey off a cliff.* "In Tanya's case, you outright poisoned her and put water lily seeds in her hand to try to subtly point the blame toward Bernard."

Mervin tut-tutted at Amy. "You amaze me, woman. Why didn't you kill Randall yourself, instead of egging me on to do it?" His face crumpled. "You made me kill my friend. I'll never forgive you for that. Ever."

Kaylee met Reese's gaze. She was right. Randall had been Mervin's intended target, not Gordon.

"You wanted to kill me, Mervin?" Randall strained against the ropes binding his legs and one arm. "Why?"

"Your stupid restaurant took every dime I had." Mervin pointed his gun at the actor. "For two cents I'd—"

Amy laughed. "Why don't you go ahead? Save me the trouble."

Blair screamed. "No don't. Please. Please don't kill him."

Mervin turned on Amy, training the gun on her. "How

about I do what I came for and get out of here? I think a couple of people might appreciate that."

"You wouldn't." Amy's face drained of color. "I'm the only one in your corner, Mervin." She reached out a hand. "I've always been there for you."

"Is that what you call it?" Mervin's eyes narrowed. "With a friend like you, I don't need enemies, right?"

"Let me go, Mervin!" Randall shouted. "I'll pay you back every dime, I promise."

Mervin tapped one foot, considering. "We may have a deal." Not that money would help him in prison, where Kaylee intended to send him.

Amy leveled her gun at Mervin. "Actually, come to think of it, I should kill you. You murdered my husband. A talented man and a real loss." Her tone implied Mervin wasn't either of those things.

"Ex-husband, you mean. And it was an accident. Not my fault."

"It wasn't my fault either. You made the decision to hit him, not me."

"Get ready to duck," Reese said in an undertone. "If they start shooting at each other . . ." He didn't need to say more. In the enclosed space, they were all at risk, especially Blair and Randall, who couldn't move out of the way.

The two killers stood facing each other, weapons ready. As Mervin and Amy eyed each other, a deadly silence descended on the room. Outside the wind continued to shriek and moan, the trees swaying and bending madly.

Kaylee heard something under the wind—a familiar clicking sound, as of tiny toenails on the floor. As she turned her head, praying she was wrong, one of the picture windows gave way with a deafening crash, broken by a huge branch. Kaylee threw herself behind the table. Glass flew everywhere. Shouts and screams mingled with the wind howling through the opening. A gun went off.

Out of nowhere, Bear launched himself at Mervin's ankles with a growl. Jocko tackled Mervin, and Reese went after Amy. Kaylee pushed herself to a standing position and raced into the kitchen. She found a serrated knife and ran to Blair and Randall.

She went to work on Randall's bonds first. Bigger and stronger, he could better help the other two subdue Amy and Mervin. With a few saws of the knife, the actor was free. He launched himself at Mervin with a roar, since he was proving to be the stronger opponent. Amy had collapsed, wailing and crying for mercy as Reese pinned her. Kaylee turned her attention to Blair and released her bonds. To her immense relief, Bear came and stood beside her, clearly uninjured.

Blair snatched up a coil of rope from the floor nearby. "Let's go help." Kaylee and the actress helped the men bind Mervin and Amy.

Once they were secure, Kaylee said, "As deputy to the sheriff of San Juan County, I'm placing both of you under arrest for murder and attempted murder."

"Don't forget arson," Mervin piped up. "I saw her set the fire."

Amy grumbled something that Kaylee was glad she didn't understand.

Kaylee added arson to the charges, then recited the Miranda Warning to them, somehow dredging it up from her memory. Her companions applauded even as Amy ranted and cried. As for Mervin, he fell silent after saying, "Justice will be done and I must submit."

Kaylee thought that especially profound until Reese said, "That's a quote from one of his movies. But quite appropriate."

Randall shook his head. "What a shame. You were one heck

of an actor, Mervin." The actor put his arm around Blair and led her into the kitchen, where the pair stood by the counters and whispered to each other. Judging by Blair's tearful yet radiant face, Kaylee guessed they were reconciling.

"I think we'd better get an ambulance here right away," Kaylee said to Reese, who was checking on Bernard. She bent behind the table and pulled out her cell phone. "By the way, I recorded everything." She played back a snippet to make sure it had worked and was rewarded by surprisingly clear audio.

Jocko reached out a hand. "I'll buy that recording from you. Name your price."

Kaylee swatted his hand and held the phone away from him. "No way. It's going to the sheriff." She checked for service, finding a couple of bars. "Who I am calling right now."

"You might not need to. We've got company," Jocko said. Through the picture window, the lights of a massive ship could be seen.

"That's a Coast Guard Cutter," Reese said, "See the antennas?"

Kaylee studied the craft steaming its way toward shore, noticing the telltale blink of the lights. That was not a civilian ship. She called Nick anyway.

"Kaylee!" Nick said, his voice urgent. "Is everything okay?"

"Sure," Kaylee said. "I mean, Amy set a fire, trying to destroy evidence, but it went out, thanks to the sprinklers. I guess she didn't know they would still work despite the outages." She took a deep breath. "We do need medical personnel here for Bernard Martin. Head injury. And you've got a couple of prisoners to pick up. Amy Early and Mervin Tuttle. I recorded their confessions, and we've arrested them and read them their rights. Oh and one more thing: as soon as you get here, I'm turning in my badge."

Bear jumped up, his feet grazing Kaylee's knees. She scooped him up and kissed his fuzzy head. "My dog and I are going home."

A week later, Kaylee rose to blue skies and unseasonably warm temperatures. Summer was having its last hurrah before autumn settled in.

"Good morning, Bear." She smiled at the adorable dog curled up next to her. After the ordeal at Mukilteo, she found herself swamped by gratitude at the smallest, simplest things. For example, waking up in her pretty bedroom with her pet. He leaped to the floor, tail wagging. "Ready for breakfast?"

At those words, he skittered toward the door, then halted, waiting for her to catch up. Kaylee threw back the covers and stood, then put on a robe and slid her feet into slippers. Together, woman and dog made their way to the bright and cheerful kitchen.

After giving Bear his breakfast, Kaylee put on a pot of coffee. As she filled the carafe with water, she noticed that the big-leaf maples were turning. The blend of yellow and green against the deep blue sky was breathtaking. After she poured the water in the coffee maker, she opened the window over the sink. Might as well enjoy the fresh air before it got too cold to have windows open.

Her cell phone rang. "Are you ready for the big day?" Mary asked. "The flowers are coming in on the early ferry. I can go pick them up if you want."

Kaylee glanced at the wall clock. "No, I'll do it. Then I'll come by the shop so we can ride together." Her belly clenched briefly in trepidation. Today a memorial service was being held at Mukilteo for Gordon, Lily, Audrey, and Tanya. The ceremony also marked the end of her work on *Flowers in the Sea*. Despite the importance of both those things, she wasn't sure if she was ready to return to the estate.

"It's going to be beautiful," Mary said. "And you'll be fine." Somehow she always picked up on Kaylee's unspoken misgivings.

"I'm glad you and the others will be there," Kaylee said. She looked at the clock again. "And I'd better get going. See you in an hour."

Kaylee showered and dressed, choosing a tea-length dress and a pair of sandals. They'd be outdoors so heels wouldn't work. Bear was invited, so she tied a new bow tie around his neck. This one featured daisies, the same flower she had purchased for the ceremony and final scene. She'd learned that Shane had let Bear out of the cabin at the dog's insistence. He'd been too dazed from his head injury to refuse. The intrepid creature had then tracked Kaylee to the Aerie.

She arrived at the docks at the same time as the ferry. She parked and got out to pick up her order. The vendor had promised five buckets of pristine white and yellow Gerbera daisies and hopefully that's what they would deliver.

Only a few passengers trudged off the ferry, and one of them surprised her. Jerry Hood, Gordon's brother. He saw her and veered from his path. "Good morning, Kaylee."

"How are you, Jerry?" she asked. "Are you going to the ceremony?"

He nodded. "Just got back from California. Seeing to Gordon's estate." He gazed out at the glittering water, as though it held answers.

"I'm sorry," she said, knowing the words were inadequate.

His tiny nod acknowledged her sympathy. Then he swung his head around, a smile crinkling his eyes. "Here on department business?"

That wrung a laugh from Kaylee. Lots of people had been teasing her about her time as a deputy. She spotted her load of flowers being carted off the boat. "No, I'm still a florist.

This week anyway."

Jerry helped her load the buckets into the back of the van, then tipped his hat and left. After making sure her flowers were secure, Kaylee headed for downtown Turtle Cove. Along with Mary, Jessica and DeeDee were at the shop.

"I brought coffee and muffins," Jessica said. "I thought we could have breakfast together." A small table where Kaylee and Mary consulted with customers was already set.

"Thanks, Jess. How did you know I was dying for a triple-chocolate muffin?" Kaylee asked. She chose a seat.

"Triple chocolate makes everything better," Jessica said. "Eat up."

For a few minutes, the women concentrated on the soft muffins and hot coffee. "Mary said that they're filming today," DeeDee said. "Does that mean Bernard is going ahead with the movie?"

"It seems so. He'll have to reshoot the scenes with Mervin, Gordon, and Tanya, though." Kaylee smiled. "Did you hear the other news? Blair and Randall are back together."

"Is that in the gossip columns?" Mary asked. "I didn't see it anywhere."

"Not yet. I had an even better source," Kaylee said. "Reese. Blair told him Bernard was sad but understood that Randall was her one true love."

Everyone laughed. "The drama of movie star relationships," DeeDee commented. "It's hard to keep up."

"That's for sure." Mary tapped her phone again. "But if the media interest in the movie is any indication, *everyone* is going to go see *Flowers in the Sea*."

"Don't forget it's going to be our screen debut," Jessica said. "The Petal Pushers and Kaylee's flowers."

"Herb had a blast at the shoot," Mary said. "The other night he told me he wants to join the local theater troupe.

Auditions are next week."

"We've created a monster," Kaylee said.

They all laughed.

A short while later, the Petal Pushers drove out to the compound, DeeDee and Jessica in her car, Mary with Kaylee in the van. A temporary bridge had been installed once the water had receded.

"It must have been something when the causeway washed out," Mary said from the passenger seat as they crossed.

Kaylee thought back to the fearsome power of the ocean waters. "It was incredible—and very frightening. The whole thing was." The gate was open, and she drove through. "I never thought I'd be back." It was only her respect for the victims that had brought her here today.

"But you are." Mary reached out and patted her knee. "And it's over. You and Reese did a good thing out here. Don't forget that."

One of the fields had been turned into a parking area, and it was almost full. Since she had the flowers, Kaylee drove right up to the beach entrance. It was showtime.

They joined the knot of attendees just before the minister started the memorial service. Jerry spoke about his brother. A well-known actress reminisced about the young actresses she had mentored: Audrey, Lily, and Tanya. Bernard gave tribute to them all, praising their talent and dedication and mourning their loss.

Afterward, Blair climbed out onto the outcropping with Randall, joined by the remaining members of the crew, including Reese and Kaylee. As Shane ran the camera and people watched from the beach, Blair tossed a handful of daisies into the water. "I will always remember you," she said. "I will never forget." The other crew members followed her lead, letting the blossoms float down to the waves below.

The flowers swirled in the surf like stars fallen from the sky. Standing next to Reese with Bear nestled at their feet, Kaylee fingered the daisy she held in her hand. Even in a time of such sadness, there was beauty to be found.

You only had to know where to look.

YOUR FEEDBACK MEANS A LOT TO US!

Up to this point, we've been doing all the writing. Now it's *your* turn!

Tell us what you think about this book, the characters, the bad guy, or anything else you'd like to share with us about this series. We can't wait to hear from *you*!

Log on to give us your feedback at:

https://www.surveymonkey.com/r/FlowerShopMysteries

Annie's® FICTION

Strands of Fate
Castle of Whispers
Secrets of the Amish Diary
Double Fudge Murder
A Novel Murder
A Fatal Arranger
The Jig Is Up